"Nothing endures but change"

- Heraclitus

DEDICATION

For Elizabeth and those who have devoted their lives to the never-ending exploration of the unknown.

Mahalo Nui Loa

Anicca

A NOVEL

ALEXANDER HOLT

Cover design and book layout by: Brendan Kearns

Visit www.alexanderholtbooks.com

PART I

CHAPTER ?

As wine is aged in a barrel — the tannins brought forward late along with rich shades of fruit, earth, and a living, breathing sensation to the palate — we delve into the early shades of this life with a virgin mind, eventually giving way to an experienced moment of clarity just before death. Like comets racing through time, we are drifters of the unknown. We earn the stars and stripes of the Americas if we're fortunate enough to experience the realms of death, love, and a white-picket smile. Yet for some, we taste the wine too soon, drink too fast, and find ourselves colliding with planets rather than basking in their beauty as we pass them by. In this part of my life, I am less aware of nouns, foreshadow, and insight and am more concerned with the verb.

Is there something wrong with the sun? What the fuck is that horrible glow shaping itself like a rainbow, its end dipped into a small root of this world we call someone else's problem? My feet apparently touch this concrete to eat, sleep, fuck, litigate, write, and realize that's all there is to it. I often wonder when these feet will gain some feeling. When will I walk for a reason and feel the cement of Sunset Boulevard? The sun is so fucking bright I forget why I moved here. Victoria was so much handier with its dim days, yet it was like watching the same parade of floats drift in the wind until someone decided to say enough was enough. That person, more often than not, was me.

Eating dry cereal with shitty coffee seems to be my job lately. In some turn of the tide, I changed my clothing from casual to *I have a bigger cock and car than you* and started having sex with the types of girls I only dreamt about and jerked off to, condom on, before college. The girls with higher standards than God, the ones who think they're better than any form of relationship out there. These are the California skanks, sluts, harlots, and whores — terms I had explicitly learned and used in grade school and unlearned in the gender studies classes I took in my first year of college. I often find myself wondering why the fuck any guy (or human, for that matter) would take such a class and attend such misinformed lectures. Yet after long, serious self-reflection and sexual discovery, I've deduced it's probably the same reason I said hi to Sandy...Sheila — or was it Sarah? That girl I banged for four and a half hours last night on the seat of my oversexed Lexus. The car still smells like cheap tricks and even cheaper pink stains.

The institution of education shall prevail, and on paper I look like a saint, donating money to the sociology department at UCLA, specifically gender inquiry, simply because I know this helps to provide a lush bouquet of blooming vagina for new freshmen. This is an attempt to add some colour to a shitty glowing rainbow that dips into all the filthy, oozing, sexually deviant holes of this city I so loathsomely call home.

I should probably backtrack my life story, my photo album if you will, for a brief moment before I begin to discuss the most intimate and degrading moments of it. In a pure, lifelong, punitive state of purgatory, my life after youth started and ended in a place called Byron Bay, situated within the overtoured, oversexed land of Australia. Sure, the place is no California, but there's more pussy there than at Hef's mansion, and the East Coast thrives off fake intimacy and borrowed dreams from the last backpacker who had a root in the same bed you supposedly just met your bride-to-be in.

Okay, her name was Marielle. Great girl — more dreams and spunk than a ten-year-old on a double trip of ecstasy and white cloud number nine. If you're wondering, yes, she had the eyes of the ocean, the body of the most beautiful swells out in the middle of the sea, a true diamond in the goddamn rough if I were to put it in layman's terms. Fuckin' oil–digging, uninspired, and illiterate laymen. This town doesn't put up with Texas, it puts up with status, and status doesn't just mean money and a comfortable place to call home. Status means me.

She and I met along the most golden of coastlines. She had everything to make a boy turn to the sunset, steal a horse and a bottle of vino, and ride until she said he was romantic enough. There are moments in life where the most fucked-up dreams come true, but one often forgets that these dreams are still dreams and that life back on the home front is more real than the infection growing on the tip of your dick. I'm glad I've shown you my cynical side because this side is all that was left in me when Marielle's ship sailed home to Norway. I moved to every place that I thought I needed to until the world turned to the dark ages — flat, with nowhere to hide.

So like I said, dry cereal for breakfast at Tiffany's every morning has left me a floppy one on more than one occasion because of this long-lost, tormenting, mind-itching, cock-blocking Marielle. God, I love her. What is love? Well, my serendipitous self-masturbatory-soothers, let me try to express this to you through the only means I know. No, it won't take up a gazillion (a number for all you laymen out there who don't know what the word *surfeit* means) pages in my photo album of love-lost images. Welcome to the overly self-indulgent life of a writer turned entertainment lawyer in the only town with enough poison to kill the heart with three words: I deep throat.

CHAPTER ?

I used to be a man of Northern Coast–inspired elegance, a man who would fashion a romantic plot, climax, and denouement within every anecdote created between my own heart and another's. In my life post-Marielle, pulling female hearts by the strings behind my carriage of lust — bodies limp and lifeless with the wear and tear of my pleasantries — then unloading and hitting the road became common practice. If you can imagine, their faces initially required very little reconstruction, their breasts always lifted enough and with subtle abnormalities, to the point where even a renowned LA plastic surgeon could find them adorable. Their personalities, well, what was usually left of them, some could say that this is where I became a voracious master in raping and pillaging the she-kind.

Like I said, before I procured this proclivity for vaginal ruination, I was a nice young man my mother's friends would orgasmically scream to the angels about. That is, until my pleasantries became too heavy for my libido-drawn carriage to pull. I began to simply fuck and trample, the horses that

5

once held their heads high in the name of love, truth, and purity while pulling my carriage of pre-filth had now established downcast faces, reluctant to look into the sky as the shame I'd brought upon myself was more than any being or beast can bare.

I may be something today, but that doesn't mean I'm anything but the faded outline of a tattered and raped shadow of what I could have been. Devoting all my blood to the cup of Christ on the day I was born wouldn't have saved me. Destined to be blasphemous, I'm a hunter with a cock for a gun, testicles filled with a white gunpowder spew tainted with pre-aborted children; a waste of chromosomes, is how I believe a scientist would put it lightly.

Like most true fairy tale endings and beginnings, it began at a club on the strip in LA where pussy had a price and golden cock rings were the norm. I had disembarked from my carriage of love-ever-after when I received a tweet from Marielle, who was currently visiting Rome:

"I need time, I need space, this world is large #gottalive #fuckyou #goodbye."

With this, I took to the strip with the intent to fuck the shit out of the world and its large qualities, which had crashed my fairy tale horse-drawn carriage right into a large pile of #mierda #shieza #shit. How's that for cultural diversity world? You #cunt.

I stumbled my way down the strip with my tongue tasting of the pavement below my feet, a soaked-in-vomit flavour made up of two-parts premium tequila and one-part street meat. I was on a solo mission to climb inside the great pink hole of outer banks LA, a feeling not dissimilar to flying into the intense vacuum of a black hole, as in "outer" space, as in a girl's asshole. My angst and despair found me in front of camera flashes that took photos of a lifelong someone who was important for something and absolutely nothing at the same time. I was at the midpoint of my law career and had become a well-established writer in the eyes of the critic, an achievement more challenging than the first time your fingerling attempted vaginal penetration, ending up analingusing its way into something you wouldn't be allowed to touch for some years to come—also as in a girl's asshole. I think I developed an anal infatuation somewhere between initial analingus and the taste of vomit-soaked concrete that then filled my mouth.

Once, in some LA club with some LA name, the LA music pulsed her hips into the rhythm and curves of the air, the lights cascaded across her fresh skin, and every man and woman in the room could taste the smell of her moist skin on the inside of their tongues. Few men or women can enter the paradise that surrounds these LA specimens of perfect pulchritude, the paradise buried deep inside these dark LA girls. My cock wandered and my face turned away from the attention drawn by every other set of mushroom-tip mongering eyes in the room. This was my challenge, my carriage, the woman I wanted to pull behind me. Fuck it, I convinced myself forever. I stood there in perfect step to the beating of my cocaine-infused heart. I stood there in perfect assumption that I had more testosterone than *Carcharhinus Leucas*, the great Bull Shark whose jawbone sat between an eighteen-carat gold frame in my law office. I stood there knowing that Marielle was staring into the night of another man's eyes. I stood there and stared into a future I didn't want. I failed to stand there as the man I once was, misunderstood and not so rational when considering fucking as a game, as a rite of passage into something more than it would ever be for me. I faltered and reflected that my feet once stood below monuments of men, great men I once aspired to become. All I could consider was a swift rebellion that would see the ending to the lives of these European conquerors of the world. Of Marielle.

The strobe lights displayed millions of the most beautiful butterflies stretching across her skin, tanned to the point of perfect desert brown and sprinkled with diamonds of the Alaskan snow. No philosophe can decipher the poignancy behind her attraction, no man or woman can even begin to understand how to peel back the layers of her libido. But I dared to, my cock dared to enter Persephone's cave.

"Hello."

You are at the mercy of your penis. If you don't believe me, you're living the biggest lie to be told since God.

"Can I buy you...?"

"Buy me?"

"Yeah, you know, who's your pimp here?" I motioned towards a large bouncer standing by the bar. She laughed. She fucking laughed.

"A drink, at least?"

She smiled, her lips turning upright at the sound of my naive yet guarded generosity. Sometimes this type of woman—most times—just wants a man to say hello. Yet most of the time we spend our spare moments taking mental Polaroids of their denim-covered vaginas and C cups—a stock pile, a hard drive in our heads filled with soft-core porn turned filthy via the avenues and primitive circuits of our grey, white, purple, blue, and black matter. We are idiots, don't forget this. Don't forget this.

"Yeah, sure. I mean, of course."

Fuck me. I was right and hopeful. She even sounded like the innocent hot girl from small town who-the-fuck-knows. Maybe I'd pay a premium for this.

This is Ayden Wallace, age thirty, just learning that the female mind isn't some preordained, hard-wired bomb that requires precise defusing by a skilled technician. There are thousands of books in every language from English to Berber on how to untangle and end the war of the cosmos that supposedly exists between man and woman. Men are not from Mars, women are not from Venus. Men are from vaginas, women are also from vaginas. Now stop being one; you were given balls, use them. Now that is a *New York Times* best-fucking-seller that no critic lost in the asshole of Coles Notes could ever put down.

This is Ayden Wallace learning that all it takes is a few broken hearts. Too much.

Gin, a lack of tonic, and voila—you're a one-man pussy wrecking crew with zero care for social norms and an affinity for social abomination. This is Ayden Wallace learning that a snowball begins in the warm virgin hands of an innocent child and ends as a weapon in the hands of a man. This is a man lost in everything, searching for anything.

"What do you do?"

The first of the three questions always asked, whether it be backpacking in Australia where you meet your love-to-never-be or at the (insert LA bar here) in a six-thousand-dollar Gucci suit. The second and third being *Where are you going?* and *Who have you come from?* The final two proverbial nails in the bondage uniform. I've learned to handle these questions with the same precision I use to deal with the spunk-soaked Hollywood harlots during my nine-to-five. The answer to progression.

We're going and *we do*.

I dare not rekindle the fuck that transpired following my first night on the strip. There are, unfortunately, no photos for my photo album that would lead to being able to remember the alcohol-induced-coma cum that filled the girl coined Stacy, who I continued to call Marielle deep into the night. Instead, like so many online photo archives, I shall describe our fuck for the entire Internet to interpret: #lick #stroke #devour #suckle #whippedcream #intruder @sallyjenkis @betsysue @allenjames #who? #wtf #moist #erect #panties #slit #precum #condom #lame #broken #whoops #father? #whocares #labium #oldschool #dildo #twodildos #lesbians? #pleasure #probing #anger #excitement #orgasm #frustration #sloppy #whiskeydick #viagra #unnecessary #vasodilation #4hours #sandpaper #vagina #success.

CHAPTER ??

I sit down to dinner with my Persephone. She floats above all the beauty in the room like an angel of darkness, eager to shame and cast the half-botoxed and botched bodies in the room back to hell. She is quiet, polite, and doesn't think like the dark angel I wish she were. She is, by all means, *the* girl you settle down with and marry, carry to cocktail parties, and put on display to shame all the legal competition in the city.

"Wow, that Ayden Wallace sure has found himself a keeper."

"That guy is so together."

That is what they would have said. But I don't let them. One simple fact hardens my appreciation and intrigue; we have already fucked three times, and I am beginning to feel the stale remains of post-bone glory. Attempt to appreciate my situation by drawing, on a chalkboard with plain, starchy white chalk, the image of a man and a woman smiling and dancing through stick-drawn flowers. I choose this image because I've graduated from love with honours in hopelessness. The image makes me vomit and turns my mouth pasty because

11

my father had a masters in war and my mother a diploma in romanticism. I scan the room as we are seated at our table, taking note of my father's teachings.

She notices the sweet smell of leather on the chairs, the fine dishes being prepared for us; she senses the money in the room and feels the warmth of comfort offered by it. I sit down and smell my office, my life, and immediately begin scanning the room for something else, something beyond this atmosphere and beyond the chalk drawing that is the current picture and frame for the Instaphoto hashtag that defines the current state of my life. And then I see an #escape.

"Forty-year-old tawny port or 2002 vintage?"

The question separates and digests the four-hundred-dollar meal I have shovelled into my stomach. I stare across the room in wonder at a perfect Spanish 10.

"Ayden, honey?"

The dreaded word *honey*. This had gone on long enough, and if I had known this girl longer than our few fucks and our dance the previous week out on the strip, she might've recognized this in my eyes. I exit to the washroom with no reply and pass by my Spanish penile conquistador, dropping a not-so-subtle touch to her skin behind my date's back. Within the milliseconds that we touch, I sense her arm hairs raise to the length that they would run if the cool Spanish air was to brush across them. Once in the restroom, I glare into the piss pot before me, undo my perfectly lubricated zipper, and expel a litre of fine wine. My thoughts begin to wander into the deep, exciting unknown of sexual promiscuity, and I can't decide if I am all of a sudden hard because of the thought of sex or of having sex with someone else.

I'm the most severe, serrated, and sharp form of asshole.

I arrive back at the table and wander my gaze over my *honey's* shoulder as our dialogue decompensates. I suddenly notice that my Spanish lover's sequins have ignited a desire beneath the sandpaper jeans that are maintaining the heart of my monogamy like a snake circling a baby. Her breasts break out of her heaven-white, string-lined blouse, which faintly reveals the outlines of her seemingly perfect areolas to the stares of all men. Her cheekbones allow her face to stretch back and reveal that Botox will not be required until age eighty-some. If one were so inclined, they would take notice of the seductive pinch between her legs that slowly moistens itself beneath the layers of her thin, now-wet Egyptian-threaded cloth, creating a moment not dissimilar to the flooding of the English locks.

Her hair is curled from root to nonsplit end, some witchcraft that had surely taken place upon her head as a rain of flowing hair broadened the scope of her sexually enveloped disposition. I forgive myself in that moment for forgetting I have this same girl from yesterday in front of me, a woman I had convinced myself was *the* girl while on a date with another woman. I forgive myself for staring into these eyes across the room and not the ones that beam with youth in front of my own fucking face. I was always doing this. I always am. Forgiving my own sins and staring into the eyes of some other future fuck, some other stars embedded within some

13

other country's skies, some worthy man's wife whom I would soon make a divorcee. I forgive myself because I can and because I have to. Try to understand me; just fucking try, you asshole.

I can taste her lips as they mush their expensive lip gloss first onto my erect membrane and then onto my lips, a seemingly homosexual performance guided by the heterosexual principals of sexual lameness and boredom. I am in Paris, I am in Spain, I am in Greece, I am having a conversation at a G-numbered summit with every country but the one in front of me.

I enter the washroom again and remove my sweater. She stands up from her table, exits, and does the same, revealing a seductive *come suck on my tight pink dessert tray* dialogue between us. Sipping a line of cocaine into my blood, I return as we both return from our change rooms and sit with our respective guileless lovers. We practise our dance like this, excusing ourselves from the bubbles of coarse reality that are our dinner tables at this Michelin-star restaurant, a restaurant that not even childhood me would have dared to dream of walking into someday. I relieve myself from this gorgeous woman that I, like all men, am tired of fucking and continue to remove layer after layer of clothing like a boy being faced with the naked female body for the first time.

"Ayden, are you okay?" my date interjects. "You seem to be pissing like a fifty-year-old woman on a road trip."

My gaze snaps quickly away from my other dining partner, leaving trails of tainted air across our table, my libido soaking the distance between my immediate maiden's physical self and my own.

"I'm fucking fine. Jesus. And don't ever compare me to your mother, the bitch." These words, these are words that childhood me never would have used. I've never even met her mother, but I'm certain she's a bitch if she pisses every five minutes. Urinary retention is the practice of sexual exploration. Try it and tell me it doesn't give you a hard-on.

Dispelling the words I had worked so hard to elicit from my maiden's lips a few evenings ago in that LA club, I take leave of my table again and pass behind her, my muse of tomorrow, brushing up against my current piece of artwork. What my date doesn't see is the swift foreign hand that reaches out from the table and squeezes my right testicle to the point where I bite my lip and hold back enough saliva to end any drought. I continue on my warpath, steadily marching into the men's room for the fifth time in thirty minutes.

I take a long look into the skin that unfolds itself around my aging insides, my bones that have begun to have feeling, my tissues that have experienced irreparable damage from the drugs and alcohol that have attempted to mend the fissures and valves of my post-Marielle heart. I stare and dream, I stare and pull my cock out, leaving just enough space between my belt buckle and zipper to entice a girl into wondering if maybe I would enjoy the pain of having my veined troublemaker defaced with the sharp, reef-like teeth of a pair of trousers — or even better, a woman's high heel. I smile inside and out in light of my ability to perform such a daunting stunt; my body is aging but my rebellion against feminism is constantly rekindled like the burning of the Olympic torch re-lit every four hours instead of every four years. I walk my willy out into the restaurant and proceed to slap the young girl's next main course right in front of her smooth Spanish-toned face.

Men and women did not speak of such blasphemy during the witch hunts of Salem. Those fuckers had a historically justifiable reason for running out of their homes naked, flailing with semen seeping down their legs from their uncircumcised urinary tracts, words of evil spewing from their lips like nothing the world's ears had ever heard. These folk had eaten turned rye bread, modern society's first fight with the free mind on naturally produced LSD. These "witches" were found guilty of pleasure and introspective discovery — that is, jizz-soaked thighs and pure images of purple-fragranced ladies dancing like monkeys in the faces of the rich. These men and women justifiably attempted to fuck the first person who matched their sexual archetype for beauty. I have no excuse other than my sexual deviance, which I had learned so much about back in gender studies. Male-dominated hegemony of my life, never leave me. (Wallace, 2014).

Comments were shared by all parties dining out that fine evening in November, but the rain that was slowly devouring the last specimens of summer outside the gold-crossed windows did not take notice. My date, my yesterday's ever after, did not plead nor beg for me, there was no diatribe, no grasp for reconciliation, mediation, or retribution, and for this I remember a trenchant fucking at the end of the evening consisting of a phalanx of my best swim team members. My piece of Spain had been swept away with her piece of man meat, which, to my demise, weighed several more ounces than mine when placed on a butcher's scale on the street of La Rambla. Sometimes the dick flop fails miserably and you're stuck with your current lover, sometimes the old you arrive with is the old you're forced to love at the end of a rainy, cold November evening. Yet sometimes you check your oddly numb right testicle before you fuck Ms. Oldie-olds and realize the pinch on your ball sack is really a thumbtack that impaled you only to display a series of digits worthy of such mutilation. She must have snuck me a fast skewer mid-dick course. My cock's capricious, cold-blooded Alaskan heart is like the ever-changing November weather, as is the desire of my unfailing love for her.

"I know what you're thinking, these things don't happen, this fucking guy and his photo album, his goddam false recollections and failing memory, his inability to create, remember, or recall real events in time, this guy, he's full of shit and ready to eat it. Well, I say to you, cocksucker, you may be correct after all, but nonetheless, fuck your pearly pink urethra aplenty…with a dull tack."

"Ayden, that's enough"

"Hallelujah." I'm #free.

CHAPTER ??

Increased respiration, chronic dilation of penile tissues, compromised judgement, a lack of reality, pupil dilation (though not quite as much as the penile sort), easily roused, borderline delusional at times, will stop at abso-fucking-lutely nothing to acquire something (even at the cost of world peace), infatuation that no psychotropic medication can cure. A clinician who admires the foundations of the *Diagnostic and Statistical Manual of Mental Disorders* would best approach treatment through the lens and the constructs of chaos theory. Whether our mind makes unconscious choices and pursues our infatuation or some cosmic deity guides our pumping red cocks into the confines of a lost wind like this world has never known, we are lost to it: always. This is our constant if there ever were an equation that boiled down the purpose of the electric enigmas that we call the mind; too simple for man to understand, seemingly too complex to ignore. Infatuation can be a prophet; it can be as simple as staring at a female's dumper for too long as if it is the only thing that is worth considering as you enter into

18

the battle of instinct versus progression. Are you your dog or are you a "human"?

This, this my friends, is the question — forget the Big Bang...well, maybe it all depends on what your taste in women is. Some prefer the slim, dirty-blonde bang with bulging hips that give way to an ass that attempts to press itself into your face, forcing you to dive deep into its warm, comforting form. I bided my time, drifting between a keen likeness to the idea of loyalty and accepting that I didn't believe in it at all. How could I when the new pussy being smushed into my childish grin every night tasted like nothing I'd ever tasted before? When lush and gushing pink lips pressed into mine and we made out as if we were at a high school dance? This was day three of the abandonment of loyalty and day three of tasting God. Might I add, God, she was always losing her heavenly flavour after day five. Give 'em just enough blood from your heart so that you can mortgage theirs and then take it back. Such are the veins life flows through in LA and the reason for the current global sexual repression.

That first night on the strip that transgressed into my first offering of a dick entrée in public set the stage for the life thereafter of Ayden Wallace. The life that would torment the cavities of every woman unlucky enough to fall within my crosshairs. Within the gushing cum of one Hollywood harlot to the other, all of which eventually went on to become one leading client after the other during their rise to fame and fortune, a star fell over the sky of night and day in LA and it was named Ayden Wallace. Ayden Wallace. Ayden fucking Wallace. Remember this name. Remember it.

What this city fails to realize, generation after generation, is that there is an undercurrent that dictates and controls the lives and Facebook walls of every starlet, harlot, producer, and director. Every social media post, every entertainment weekly, every smile, and every tear is passed through the locks of law. We pursue the glamorous tweeners, tweeters, and twat-twiddling Oscar runner-ups and rise to the platform of a stardom that outlives the plastic-wrapped lives of the best Brad Pitts and Madonnas. We own this town, and we are always ready to write a script with an ending that kills and bills any character who gets in our way. We direct the directors by controlling production companies, we make use of Latin to peel the clothes off fresh eighteen-year-olds when the cameraman begins a new reel and the key grip jerks off to the images he's seen backstage next to the maintenance and special effects carts. We own his cock just like we own the tits that draw the splurge from it. I can tell that you're beginning to see Ayden Wallace as a Type A narcissist with sociopathic tendencies, but please try to comprehend the power I have to deal with every day knowing that I have a key grip on the key grip's dinger.

It's powerful shit, man.

"Ayden, hey."

Fuck me, it's the Mexican.

"What's up, immigrant, papers and documentation please."

This guy, what a fucker, I love him.

"Getting old, amigo."

"You were actually born eight months and three days before me, Ricardo, which means that

20

your dick has three more wrinkles than mine as professed by true evidence in the latest *Men's Health*. And, I know that you're not circumcised, so add another five years' worth of snakeskin fuck face," I say, readying to further a defence against absolutely anything he says to me. Over time, I will learn to control this urge to defend and destroy every human I meet...slightly.

"Okay, man, take it easy. Was just wondering if you'd like to join us for lunch at the mercado de —"

I roll my eyes at his accent and can tell he knows exactly what I mean.

"You'll never win a court case with that tone, Mr. Elegance, not even a B-list actor one."

"All right, man, lunch or no?"

I'm a difficult person to be around, I get it.

"Yeah, give me ten, I have to wrap up this case with some rapper."

"Another name drop? What did they do this time, kill someone? Fuck something weird? Insult —"

"Shut the fuck up, I'll be right down." I can feel his confidence in his humour building and it requires an immediate cock slap.

I shuffle through my mahogany desk drawer. The smell is enchanting but I have come to ignore it. The entire room smells of sweet leather and rich wood, the kind of wood that if burned would draw the attention of every Catholic pope-follower on social media. I flirt with the idea of calling my secretary in for a quick line and a blow jizzy, but I am distracted by a piece of paper my fingers feel, taste, and smell at the back of the drawer. An emotion protrudes my adult mind and digs deep into the chasms of my adolescent mind. *Marielle*. This is a

21

smell I cannot ignore. I have stored her letter in the back of my drawer and my consciousness, which has served only to preserve the perfume she has aptly sprayed on every letter she has ever sent to me. I gain the feeling of full cardiac arrest in my chest. I don't need to open it, I already know what it contains. The content isn't so much important as is the taste of nostalgia on the tip of my tongue. My entire body tastes the presence of the letter, and for a moment, Marielle preoccupies all time, space, and matter. She propels herself into my consciousness like an African child throwing a stone through a tourist's car window. *Smash!* The glass shreds my pupils and sucks the pigment out of my irises, it scrubs the colour from my artificially bronzed skin like 40-grit sandpaper on butter. It fills my inner and outer ears with a white noise so loud that it affects my balance, like a tightrope walker losing sight of the platform ahead, looking down into vertigo and certain death.

My body falters and ages my caffeine- and cocaine-stricken heart another five years; if I were over fifty, I would be in full cardiac arrest. My teeth chomp down and grind ivory into ivory (my dentist always says I should wear a mouth guard twenty-four seven; the comment is legitimate, especially now). I reach into my desk for a pill of Marielle-be-gone, searching it out of a hidden compartment at the back of my desk. A small notch with a finger hold just large enough to fit the middle or index finger holds my respite. I pull it to the left and slide the mahogany aside, fingering for the tiny pill with my thumb as if I am trying to stretch the asshole of a virgin before some anal bump-bump. I find the spot and press my thumb down, pulling out a piece of ecstasy and placing it into the dark chamber of my whiskey-moistened mouth. I'm ready for lunch.

Lunch is a gathering of the bulls that parade the streets of Spain in search of blood and, with some luck, human excretion if the victims of our duty ended up totally fucked. I sit across the table from some young would-be entertainment lawyer who speaks as if he is reinventing the Latin language. In most situations, I would reach over the table with my dick out and lay one on this young son of a bitch, but between my Marielle-be-gone pills and my other pending lawsuits, I decide just to tell him that his thoughts on the current importance of a new, more definitive social media and intellectual property contract framework for our firm are worth half a peasant's sperm at a sperm bank. Everyone laughs, even him, because if he doesn't he knows that I will find him once my current lawsuits are settled and *SLAP* will go my cock into his pupil. Try explaining that to your mother over Thanksgiving dinner.

For the record, I have and actually do cock slap; it is an art form that can be used only by men of my calibre and prestige. Mostly because of this formula: humour + anger / monetary cost = I'm rich and don't give a fuck and it's fun so I do it. *SLAP*!

"Amigo, what's the deal with the Bernadette case? I've heard there are some illegitimate circumstances that have come up and that your witness may be discredited."

My eyes shoot across the Perrier and hundred-year-old Châteneuf-du-Pape.

"Where did you hear that?"

My skin begins to feel the water beads that drip down the side of the Perrier bottle in front of me, and I don't like it when my skin feels.

"Speculation, mainly, but someone at Parkson & Lawson mentioned that you might be in for a rough go this afternoon."

I feel the entire bottle of Perrier pouring down the insides of my shirt.

"I hope you know what you're talking about, because I'm about to turn this town upside down."

Storms in the middle of Tennessee don't move this fast. I throw a wad of cash on the table, which is probably enough to feed a family for a month in Senegal, and push my way through the pulsing blood inside of my body as the anti-Marielle pills run their course in creating the physical experience of walking through molasses. I know a guy, people like me always know guys, and if there is ever someone doubting the legitimacy of my case or questioning the authenticity of my wines, he helps me make it authentic, he helps make the judge indulge me and buy my story, he helps make me *me*.

CHAPTER ????

My afternoon finds me surrounded by suits in a boardroom flat fuck in the middle of another hot, pathetic-looking raped Angeles day. My eyes are less than sharp tacks and my mind is even duller, though I smile through it with confidence that my legitimizer has settled my current witness issues. I look at my clamped knuckles and realize I've forgotten to wash my hands of the all-too-familiar smell of a midday stand.

Ricardo flashes me a look and an even sharper stare with that damn diamond that resembles some small fortune in Liechtenstein pierced through his right ear. I have told him time and time again that I want to cock punch him every time I see him because of that earring, but he insists that it's a statement. *Yeah*, I always say, *a statement that you would like two little boys to gang bang you between the confession chamber and the altar. This is America, muchacho, not Mexico.* I know what this look means. It means that I have either (a) forgotten the right documents or (b) forgotten to take a condom off my dick and it's hanging through my zipper.

I lean backwards and check under the table, realizing that amidst the Wheaties and shitty coffee I had this afternoon, I've forgotten to lose the treasure I'd tried to put on some poor girl's chest after dealing with my legitimizer. I excuse myself without looking for any reply and walk out the boardroom door, covering my junk with the new case statistics of some Hollywood star who was caught drunk driving while I was having sex with what resembled a seventeen-year-old girl from Santa Monica. I assure you that she was doused in the aftermath of chemical combinations from a Paris laboratory that made the tip of my sex drive tingle, "tested on animals" and used on the same. I should be reading this case report, instead I am using it to cover the condom that hangs from my dick like a stocking left out for Santa . A stocking that a drunk, alcoholic father had filled with milk instead of chocolate and candy.

I walk down the hallway into the neon-lit, stainless steel washroom that is an apt description of every day I've worked for this law firm, which the papers call the real director of Hollywood. The bathroom stinks, which is weird because usually there is a Mexican bloke who cleans it for twenty cents an hour and smiles at me every day just for saying hello in Spanish. *Hola, amigo. mi pene es muy grande. ¿Como estas?* What a joke. Two million a year, and I still walk into what resembles a residence washroom back in Victoria. I take off the condom Santa left me on his off night and wash my hands with the fifty-dollar-a-bottle soap that we apparently need in order to stay healthy and professional. Healthy? Maybe. Professional? Tell that to those starving in a place called *This Firm Doesn't Fucking Care*.

Ricardo is still giving me that shit-eating grin filled with angst when I walk back into the room, and it gives me the feeling that he would fuck anyone in the room at that exact moment, even my boss, Lars Mortinson, who I am already sure he has fucked twice to get that earring he is wearing. What a faggot. And yes, this brings me to the word *faggot*. I still use this elementary-entitled word, but only for my counterpart and favourite lead cocksmuggler. Might I add, since my entire photo album is now on display, that I am also somewhat of an artist on the side, the type who creates pieces to gain access to the more literate fans of Los Angeles propaganda. I create works that challenge World War II book-burning advertisements, and I burn the title *City of Angels* with literary burning bags of doggy poop.

"You need a maid to dress and clean up after you, amigo?" Ricardo says to me by the coffee maker that shines like a fake sun, knowing surely that there is a joke about his cousin or mother coming in his general direction.

"Sorry, Ricardo, I'm not as lucky as you to have a boyfriend like Lars Mortinson to suck me off after I blow my juice. Or maybe he's the one who does the pumping and you take…that would explain why you would never run into this same situation," I remark in a tone that I would use if I were prosecuting some obese movie star.

"That earring still looks gay, amigo," I say, finishing my speech and making a half attempt to pull it out of his ear. Ricardo gives me an awkward look and then gives me a Mexican hug and asks how

I've been outside of the stress he had induced within me over lunch. I tell Ricardo the same old shit and that I had a dream about Marielle again last Friday that just won't leave me alone. I tell him about my asshole agent who has been pushing me to come out with new material and how I can't focus on anything but this itch, not only on my dick but also in the back of my internal dealings, that strongly resembles Marielle's touch on my skin. The waves that lap this smoggy shoreline are dreaming that they picked a better final resting place.

Aren't we all.

CHAPTER ??

Walking down the hallway, I smile to myself in self-aggrandizing glory as I pass two — or was it three? — interns that I have already laid my genetics on. Face? Or was it back? One of these days it will be inside one of them and I'll have myself a nice boy. This thought dissipates just as quickly as it enters my mind when I see Lars waiting in my office for me.

"Wally, my boy!" Lars vomits the words from his mouth like a man trying to connect with his bastard son after twenty years of displacement from his life. You see, Lars is a great barrister, a decent husband, and a good father, from what I could tell when I was over at his house banging his twenty-year-old daughter. However, the one area he lacks in is his social confidence outside of the courtroom. The motherfucker wants to be me in every way, and I cannot say that there is anything else in this world that makes me want to cut my own dick off and shove it down my own throat more. Niceties only go so far when you have a beagle following you around sniffing your ass, trying to decipher what kind of shaving cream you use to rid your asshole of the hair that every postmodern hipster claims they weren't born with.

He really is a one-of-a-kind, enjoyable pain in the ass, I think as I say enthusiastically, and somewhat condescendingly, "Lars, my good man, how goes the struggle through the haze that is the Los Angeles dream?"

"Well, I've got good news, Wally, great news. News that will make you, how do you say it? That way that always makes me laugh, you know, Wally…"

He is waiting for me to make some off-the-cuff comment that one would read in one of my novels.

"Fucking enlightening," I reply with a smirk two-year-olds make when they shit their diapers.

"Ah ha! You are true blue, my friend. When's the next novel?"

Jesus, not him too. I bite my tongue. "It's a work in progress. I need some inspiration, you know how these things go."

The world is a tough place to live in when humans, of all things, hang off your every word in hopes of being the first to indulge in the next greatest epiphany from the lips of a modern Californian messiah. I'm the great saviour of those left hopeless and drowning in the American sundrenched dream that is every west coast of the world. I'm the great liar of our time, or at least one of them.

"Well, I for one am….jonesing! for your next novel. But hey, let's get down to business here."

I am waiting for a briefing on a new case or for a lecture on something that I had missed in a current one—anything that will imply that he is here to do business outside of trying to suckle my man twat. Unlike most junior partners in this same situation, I want to be reamed out over an affidavit or deposition gone wrong. Instead, we are done.

Lars—big old fat fucking Lars with his red hair, lofty nose, glasses that make him look like a psychiatrist, four-year-old freckles, and stubby legs—walks out of my office with that usual swagger rich Californians have. He strolls out my door and down the glass-lined hallway, overly satisfied in the short exchange of words that has occurred. As always, Lars leaves my sight with high hopes that I will use his latest dumb-fuck word of the day in my next novel. Today's is *jonesing*. The fucker. The *Oxford Dictionary* lacks the insight to describe a word as sickening as the aftertaste in my mouth after our pre-cum-infused, unfriendly verbal engagement. Humans; always trying to find some way to sneak into fame, even if it's just one fucking word in a novel read by those who will spend their afterlives in purgatory with no other final destination than hell.

***

"I fucking hate it when he does that," I complain to Ricardo in the café that sat like an ancient moai in my life across from the glass building that was the brain of Hollywood. "I fucking hate how he just stops into my office like he fucking owns it or something. It's like walking into someone's house and kicking your feet up on their sofa and programming their goddamn TiVo."

"Like walking into someone's house and fucking their twenty-year-old daughter…yeah, I hear you, amigo," Ricardo snaps back with sheer self-satisfaction, reminding me of how privileged he is to know the stories locked in the dark chasm of my loins.

"I don't do that every day, amigo…c'mon."

I laugh as I sip down my overpriced latte. The top froth resembles a mosaic of the DNA I have wasted on this world, it stares back at me with every sip I pull into my mouth. With this thought, I place down my cup, gag slightly, and tell Ricardo of my plans for the evening, which will consist of a glass of fifty-year-old Chivas Royal Salute and a pen—a pen that I still needed to pick up from Nils's office. As thoroughly responsible as these plans may have been, they are met with perfectly calculated and expected redirection.

Ricardo has a special treat planned for us, which is sure to please every immediate desire in my body from head of cock to toe. Our extracurricular conversations have become a conditioned response in my life, a distraction from the boring moments of litigation and a stimulus that almost always elicits a hard-on in my pants. Pavlov proved that dogs would salivate when prompted with a bell that was soon followed by food. Ricardo is my bell, and it sings one tune: "It's time to eat some pussy."

CHAPTER ?

If I were sitting in a hospice, retirement home, or psych ward for the elderly and mentally unstable, I would spew my story into the ears of men and women who, if not already deaf, would become the vulgarity that describes my life and actual self. If there were a man who had no recollection of his own story, he could enjoy and take pleasure in the fact that he could be told such a grotesquely comedic story and not have to bear the scars that come with it. I was once a kind, gentle young man with intentions to save the heart of man from people like me. I was once in a woman studies class — and not just to meet women. To this man who may or may not appreciate my story in this bright white room (which could possibly be where my alveoli suck in the last entrails of oxygen my body uses for considering at what age is too old to jerk off to "barely legal" pornography), to him I say, "Live my story, because it's who we all are at the core. Animals, barbarians, sex hounds, cannibals with Darwinian progression. Cannibals who have learned that just sucking on a woman's labia can actually taste better than eating it. Literally. This is us. Tell me if you can handle this truth when you consider that your current story may not be real."

CHAPTER ??

A sailboat uses the wind to travel and the sea to explore. I use a Lexus, a hot blade of oil, and a personality that would make the Queen of England wet. Sex is a phenomenon, like grass growing or like the Macy's Thanksgiving Day Parade — each float, one after the next, offering a different tactile piece of stimulation, a different image, and sometimes, if you're lucky, a little piece of happiness.

Sunset Strip is always a treat when you're loathing the status of your love life. The atmosphere reflects the libido of every man who wishes they had a place to put their juice, and the cars make tourists wonder if God employs half the people in LA. *Fake* is a general term and a term I've come to accept as ideal. In LA if you're not fake, you're poor; and if you're original in style, you won't be getting laid until Pharrell decides to copy said style.

I pull up to the Tropaviaro club in my unoriginal suit, with my unoriginal fake Australian accent that I use to make panties fall at my feet. Again, I wear unoriginal because I don't want to fuck with Pharrell. I see Ricardo talking to two prospects, one dressed in a yellow piece of cloth and another dressed in what I can only describe as nothing. Ricardo calls me over and I tell the girls that I'm from Byron Bay, Australia, and that I'm richer than God himself. Both girls recognize me, having probably read my novels and seen me in the papers and on television. Nonetheless, they pretend that I'm Wooza from Australia and we enter through the VIP doors in the back.

I always wish that I am a different man, a man of purpose and a man who can appreciate the legs of a gorgeous woman as they tremble against his, lips tasting like the salt from the most beautiful shoreline, a body that makes the hills of Scotland jealous.

"Time for some tequila, you fuck ass! *Ahuevo!*" Ricardo calls belligerently from the VIP bar.

I stumble up to the bar with my new piece of salt to fill my wound left by Marielle. As we say cheers to another drunken night, to the beginning of a new multimillion-dollar court settlement about nothing of any importance, and to the bodies of our part-time lovers, my part-time happiness, which the tequila brings out, is stirred and shaken, much like an astronaut who disturbs the stars.

Marielle, the girl who walks into the bar with her back turned to me, the girl who strikes a pose on the red carpet, the girl who fights off injustice as a district attorney, the girl who always turns around and is never there.

"So what's good word, man? The place is crawling with starlets and we're both rolling higher than Heffner in twat, yet I see that look on your face and I just really want to either rub my nut sack all over it or force-feed you some labium."

"Yeah, you always know."

The music feels as if it's growing louder, stronger by the second, and the overstimulation is leading my brain into a rare state of dysregulation.

"Gin?"

"Oh yes, gin, the substance of clarity."

The bleached fluorescent purple and pink lights flicker against the granite bars and suffocate the vibrant colours on suits that are made to impress even under such porn-appropriate lighting schemes. One central bar is the hub for those middle-upper class civilians lucky enough to bullshit their way into the club. These are the guys who have to try to pull pussy into their mouths and onto their cocks; these are the men who have to fight like bleeding chickens in Thailand for their female ejaculate shots. Those of us who line the less populated and 250-pound-bouncer-protected VIP bars elevated above all the middle-class ruts simply have to ask for some squirt as if we are only asking for a shot of tequila at an all-inclusive in Cancun. *One shot of the brunette with the big naturals, please.*

The majority of the volume comes from speakers that hang over the entire club, dragons protecting the firm and falsified "club love" ideology that nightclub owners fight to protect and keep alive because they can't keep themselves properly alive. They do this until the energy drink vodkas slowly kill their hearts into piles of melted black tar and they retire working on the shores of Santa Monica, realizing that beachside bars are where it's been at all along. If I had revelations like this on my dying day in some bed in some white room, I would end my life sooner rather than later with a shotgun to the noggin.

The pathetic epiphanies held within LA clubs are beyond my comprehension. This is why I sip on free poon juice whenever the fuck I want while the blue-collar pillbox soldiers fight below me for it until the death.

The remainder of the volume comes from the large stage, which is decorated with the finest colours that can currently protrude the human cornea. Every year these clubs are coming up with new ways to penetrate our fovea and provide a new stimulus for our amygdalae, hoping to elicit new and more poignant responses to the things we experience within their sanctuaries of sex, drugs, and current electro-rock shit. Three women stand on stage, each with a drum in front of them and a big rubber black dick in hand. They alternate hands as they flip their great phalluses upside down in the air, tossing their big, juicy-with-rubber cocks back and forth in some odd Papua New Guinea–ritualistic fashion. The sexual envelope we humans push is always retrograding.

It's all sexual deviance that we humans have done before. As we "advance," we declare acts such as public coitus to be social blasphemy only to make it the next edgy video on TMZ one thousand years later once Pharrell gets hold of the idea. Take the tribes of Sambia who still suck the living-flesh dildos of their elders to the sound of phallic flutes; compare that to these bitties banging dildos on drums, and you've got yourself a cross-sexual analysis representing how repressed we, the advanced and refined, actually are. It's pathetic, really, and it doesn't faze me. I glare with pity at the black dildos striking drum skins, wondering, for a moment, if I am of Sambian descent.

With a dance and fifteen gin and tonics, I am well below the level of any professional porn star — getting me hard, let alone getting me home, would take rocket science. The air is warm but unsettling, and the moon is winking at two lonely assholes inside one of the most luxuriously defined clubs in the world. We walk into the washroom, where you can always find cocaine dashed across the mirrored counters, people fucking and getting sucked in bathroom stalls, and the guy no one likes taking a shit. Some things can't be changed by socioeconomic status — addiction and public shitting are two of the more commonly underappreciated behaviours.

I look up into a perfectly crafted mirror, which has been replaced since the last time I was here, staring into myself and pulling my fingers down my frown lines like most lawyers do, even if they are successful. The mirrors, the lighting, the artwork, the air is always being changed and recycled here, there is always something new and more fascinating to stimulate yourself with. It is why we polygamists so aptly love the fuck and flee — the women may as well be hung on the walls as art in this place because the turnover is staggering. I have fucked three women in one night within this club at a speed that no artist of any painting capacity could keep up with. This is how I like things.

Ricardo asks me to go back to his flat in Holmby Hills with the two girls whose names I still cannot remember for the life of me. The music pulses my temples and I try to remember if the story I am telling is a story I've told before and I begin to question the birth numbers on my driver's licence. I don't know if it's the air or the gin that leads me to consider some option other than sex, but as I look towards the open air above us in the restroom, I choose that something else.

We exit the restroom and approach our two pieces of modern art.

"I'm good, amigo, you go, and you know what that means."

I give Ricardo a wink and the two girls giggle and grab his cock and ass as though foreshadowing the routine they will perform on him in his multimillion-dollar place he calls La Deja Casa. I grab my emotions, which are starting to seep out from my subconscious, and aimlessly hail a cab and ask him to take me to the ocean. With liquor bound to my breath like a dull knife to a borderline's wrist, I flop into the cab and whistle away at the side of my happiness, which will never quench its thirst for reality.

CHAPTER ???

The cab smells as if it has spent the night in Chino or riding the strip of Crenshaw, its leather sticky with a filth that the youth inside me can giggle at before the lonely elder shoves a fist to his face and says, *Be disgusted.* My guide for the evening is barely visible behind his black cap, which shines with pleather and studded metal tacks, and the cheap smell of deep-fried trans fat further provides an obvious separation between my perfectly trans-fat free body and his own. He must've been in Chino.

The drive feels endless as blurred visions of palms, distress, love, and loathing pass me by out the passenger window. Ziggy Marley sings of walking on a beach in Hawai'i, a song which begs me to think *Where the fuck am I?*, but then a surge of philosophy overtakes me, a tongue that speaks in drunken slur but somewhat resembles words regarding the fact that it doesn't even matter. The cab driver pulls up into what I believe to be the Santa Monica area, and I drop my Visa at his feet and make a joke about how he is probably getting drunk off my breath and shouldn't drive anymore. I don't know how much money it cost me to get to where I am, but I do know that to someone who doesn't have much it's a lot. I can feel the crashing waves beating against my chest, and it reminds me of Sombrio, The Mentawais, Snapper Rocks, Bondi, Chicama, and all the other places I've surfed in my life, the places I went to see in order to keep Marielle off my mind before I discovered self-medication and law. I haven't spoken with the ocean in over two years, haven't heard its voice or ridden it until we have nothing left to say to each other. Today it is expensive suits and cheap conversation that keep me occupied, and in this moment I feel Marielle surging into my heart, pressing on it and trying to resuscitate me. I once sailed a boat from Oregon to somewhere and got lost in the rip currents, washed ashore an island that displayed to me the wonders of everything I then did not have. Whether I did or I didn't, it's a nice story in my mind, and I plunge my face out of the cab and into the black night with emotions spilling from my every pore like a pedophile sweating in a supermall.

I know in this moment that I'm Pavlov's dog, hearing and smelling the ocean, waiting for Marielle to arrive. This is why I've strayed so far from the ocean: it is more salt to fill my wounds, more than that beautiful fucking slut that I could be inside. I think about Ricardo and the pink that must be in his mouth right about now. His face dripping with the cum of an angel in disguise, probably a nice girl at heart who just happened to fall in with the wrong crowd — the crowd that I represent every day and bail out of jail on terms that are exceedingly fucking ridiculous, terms that no one in the world would get away with unless they had a name that is television popular. Cum, money, drugs, and a life that I call my own. I take a joint out of my pocket and light it with more fire than I have left inside my heart. I hold the lighter up into the night sky and the writer in me sighs. As I write the words *Believe, don't just belong* against the warm, airy canvas, I pass out, and the night steals my mind as a bum steals my money.

CHAPTER ?

I wake up with nothing on me but a belt and a fancy suit that I tear from my body in frustration. My wallet, watch, and everything artificial on my body is missing, and I've never felt simultaneously better and worse in my life. It is the bare bones now, survive or be lost—a thought as juvenile as they come to a well-travelled man. The chemicals in my brain begin to balance themselves out again, and my step begins to tread into a pattern that is less like a drunk Irishman and more like the swagger of, well, myself. I look for options and find my sense of humour, so I do what I do best: strip my self naked and walk down Palisades Beach Road, knowing that no matter what lawsuit may be thrown my way, I will have it beaten by sundown. The looks pass my smile, some in disgust, some filled with anxiety, and finally after a total of five minutes, one pulls over.

"Hey, Aydan Wallace, right?" The words come from a red Camaro with an interior that is far superior to that of the cab I took last night.

"That would be my face's name, want to learn what other names I have?" I respond as I look down at my cock, which I've been hiding behind a piece of driftwood.

"Only one other, get in."

I wind up back at my personality's birthplace in Beverly Hills, a very postmodern pseudo Jon Jerde design if he were to create a small-scale home rather than the Bellagio. Its trim is bursting at the seams with a white as vibrant as the house of white in Washington. My driveway is the devil's gateway to hell, beautifully designed to fool any woman into thinking that it is a refuge for stranded vagina with daddy issues. My lawn is manicured to the perfection of the rolling hills of Ireland, and the brilliant windows throughout the house, which forecast the weather with their 360-degree views, are somewhat of a marvel to those first years at USC who occasionally stroll the neighbourhood in search of ideas to steal for their final architecture projects. I can disclose the fine detail that makes up the insides of the house — detail so well perfected as to hold a presidential dinner — or the uniqueness found within the very nonunique infinity pool concept on the roof, but I prefer, as always, to discuss the real material that gives character and rise to the place: me.

The girl this time is named Rayna. Her perfume smells like she has an overpowering father, a dog named Francesca, and a desire to fuck the shit out of a famous anything. I tell myself I need to ignore the throbbing tumour I have on top of my neck and stick my cock where she wants it. The last thing I need is what happens next.

In a final act of appreciation for the ride home with this rich, sociopathic nympho, I go down on her and pretend I'm eating a mouthful of food at a free brunch after being trapped on an island for three months, an adventure I still cannot remember if I was a part of in some other life story. I feel her tightening up inside and prepare for her to cum when I receive a mouthful of apple juice for dessert. I realize now there is a consequence for fucking girls who pull over on Palisades with their legs opened wider than my own gates of hell.

I snap back with a look of excitement and disgust on my face. A beaming grin leads her to believe I enjoyed being hosed down like a urinal at a horse race. I take a deep breath and pick up her clothes, throwing them and the words *I'm more of an orange juice kind of guy* onto her. Embarrassed, slightly amused, and definitely still wanting my cock, she pulls her high heels on, breaking one in the motion, and hobbles out my front door like a wounded camel running for water in the middle of the Sahara. Jesus Christ, it's time to write. I drag a cigarette off the glass side table, which balances an impressive collection of sex toys on it, ones I'm not familiar with. I light a cigarette, pull my robe around myself, and step out onto my oceanfront patio, which overlooks what is to most Californians a fresh start and which to me is a bleak reminder that even in moments of pure beauty, there is sexual deviance present.

This excites me into doing one thing: breathing.

CHAPTER ??

I can't eat and I'm starving, I can't sleep and I'm exhausted, so I grab a pen and strive to force out some romantic bullshit that Nils wants on his desk today. The smell of piss lingers, ingraining itself in my senses as I write the first letters on a blank page: P-A-L-I-S-A-D-E-S. I know that ninety-nine point nine percent of the people who read this novel will think I'm discussing the long-lost love of my life and will never for a moment think I'm naming the book after some sadistic bitch who pissed in my corn flakes. Literally.

After several long hours of strife trying to force out a hit that will somehow magically make a million more pounds of pussy arrive at my door, I take a quick shower and clean my ass with my thirty-thousand-dollar bidet. This bidet is no ordinary bidet, it is made from Kurt Cobain's toilet, which I conveniently bought from his ex-lover when she was selling off his entire life just to keep her ego in the market.

I hit the studio lights on my way out of the house and they drift down into darker and darker shades, a form of light dimming that the world's leading industrial organizational psychologists researched and choreographed either to please CEOs and relax them at home or to relax and motivate their sweatshop workers in third-world workshops. I grab my platinum cellphone, which was given to me by a famous someone, the background image a perfect picture of her naked self. Yes, she does check to make sure I don't change it, but only on Wednesdays when I have time between my eleven and my twelve o'clocks.

I jump into my car and pull out of the driveway only to hear a woman scream. I slam on the brakes. "What the fuck now. What. The Fuck. Now."

I have Picassoed some cat's insides across the pavement (this poor woman would have rather seen my famous someone's open asshole, believe me). Another moment of my surreal life to sigh at and eternally blind myself to the sickness that the moment has caused someone else.

Immediately after I yell out my words of wisdom, I see the woman is old — much too old to fuck more than once. I correlate this epiphany with the reflection that I am probably in the wrong as I have killed her cat. The next immediate thought I entertain is that I am never wrong. I am Ayden Wallace. And I am going to show this bitch what I am made of.

"Sorry, ma'am, but I think it's a little late to be walking your cat, this is your fault, dontcha think?" I say it in a soft manner, pretending I didn't just call her a bitch with the tone of my sound waves.

"You sorry asshole, you killed my baby! She's dead! Mary, Joseph, and Paul, oh my, you have taken my baby, oh my, may the Lord cover his eyes to such a sight. The blood! Please, God, no— It's only noon, what do you mean it's too late to walk my cat!?"

I attempt to process the urgently developing situation. Fuck me, I do not want to be engaged in this dialogue about a dead species I despise, this piss on my breath is about to give me a nosebleed, fuck this and fuck her.

"Well, darling, what I mean is, cats are called pussycats, they are like pussy—don't let them out of the house past 6:00 a.m., and if you give them too much leash and let them get too ahead of you, they get hit by a car...usually its unintentional, but sometimes it's because I hit them. I really don't fucking care about your cat, and my mouth currently tastes like the excrement that is now scattered across the tarmac and stuck to the rims of my Lexus. For the love of all those fucking religious names you just spewed, keep your next one on a leash." The situation of stray, dead pussycat paralleled the fuck juicing that had just occurred on my face for breakfast. I have consummated juicing pussy to the level of a skilled master.

I stare her down and realize for the fifth time this week that I may truly, possibly, be the worst human being on earth; yet I'm happy I excel at something that most don't. I throw a cheque in her face and tell her that if she wants to sue me she can find my number on the front of every billboard from Oregon to Arizona. Wow, I really am a prick; I wonder what happened to that word *love* all those years ago? Oh yeah, lost it in the dryer along with those other lines that said I would find it someday.

Pussy juicing; it has a ring to it. I may be on to something of literature-related value.

The sun is a dragon breathing such a fierce amount of heat on my hair that I can't even see straight. With the mix of hangover, dead cat blood, drying urine, and this heat, I feel like Oprah Winfrey on a book tour in Uluru. I pull over to grab a bottle of water at the gas station and realize I'm late for my meeting with my agent again. I swoop into the store, grab an overpriced quadruple-osmosis-processed water, and go for my wallet, which I soon realize is in the dirty palms of some street rat kid I would've pitied years ago when I was considering social welfare policy as my direction in law. How's that for karma?

Well, the funny thing about karma is that it's dated and doesn't realize that a face as beautiful as this gets even better-looking girls to pay for his anything. I thank the girl who yells out, "It's Samantha!" as I jump the door and land in the seat of my car. Hmm, Samantha. I would name my daughter that if I had one…shoulda fucked her. The Lexus engine grumbles from the heat and I tell her to chill the fuck out or she'll be hitting the wreckers. Cars are like women: they don't really give a shit and won't change unless you put more money into them.

I tear down the freeway, smelling that sweet salt air I reconciled with last night. I try not to think about the regret I used to feel when I would wake up in the morning after banging a high school sweetheart in my parent's bed while they were away on vacation. Yet all my regrets seep back into my conscience anyway, so I light a cigarillo and hit the accelerator, preferring to taste the urine still coating the back of my palate rather than sip my hydrogen-oxygen beverage.

The drive seems endless, and I feel sweat seeping through the armpits of my Gucci suit. I have plenty more Gucci, but it's just such a hassle to change before a meeting. Five miles before my exit I see lights flashing in my rear-view, so I pull over into the far right lane, hoping the cop is passing me in favour of some asshole driving faster than eighty miles an hour in a sixty. The cop follows me into the right lane, and as I lack the adrenalin for a good chase that would get me mass publicity, I pull over and decide to take the reins of the high horse this cop is riding on.

"Licence and registration, please, Mr...?"

"Wallace, it's Ayden Wallace."

"Yes, Mr. Wallace, loved reading about your approach on that last legal suit."

"I'm a soothsayer, what can I say." I do my best to paste an awfully homosexual look on my face.

"Sorry, Mr. Wallace, even though my daughter will kill me for giving you this ticket instead of getting an autograph, justice must be served."

If you let me meet your daughter, I will serve justice all over her face.

"Yeah, well, what can you do? Guys like you don't make that much, gotta pick at every last penny you can find."

The cop gives me a cocksmuggling look and leans his jolly fucking Green Giant shoulders over my car door as if he has more rights than I do. "I'll let you off this time with a seventy in a sixty, but remember, the law doesn't forget."

51

I feel obliged to laugh and remind him, as I would a child, that I am the leading lawyer for a very, very popular law firm and that if he continues to mention how he is going easy on me, I will take note of his badge number and make it a priority at my firm to breach him on harassment charges.

I'm the single strongest Spartan warrior screaming in the face of a Persian, yet I receive a ticket for eighty in a sixty and drive away with my tail between my legs.

Fuck it, I need to hit this meeting. I'm late, and Nils has a temperature so constant it makes the sun jealous.

CHAPTER ??

My parking spot is full but I have no time to complain. I park in the stall next to it and grab my notes on *Palisades*, which I wrote in the midst of my dwindling, piss-soaked memory of this morning, and I rush into Sync Publishing with a hard on that would put Jack the Ripper to shame. I don't really know why I have this erection and I consider that maybe I'm a piss fiend. This thought diminishes as I walk through the glass door and behold the stubby Englishman who is not scared to anal probe a camel in the middle of Sudan if it means making money.

"You fucking lazy-ass, tea-bagging son of a bitch," Nils says. "You're late, but I don't even care, it's just amazing to see a face as glorious as yours in my office."

Something is off. Nils is never this happy—he wasn't even this happy when I signed a contract that stated that if I ever fucked his wife I would give him all my assets. What can I say, the guy knows me very, very well.

"What's up, Nils? Everything all right?"

"You bet it's all right, we're getting the go-ahead for a novel-to-film release that needs to be written, edited, produced, and on the shelves by March 12 of next year."

This is where the conversation turns from a family movie to a Tarantino flick.

"Nils, you over-greased, pre-released cunt, I thought I was out of that film shit. It's January and I have half a page of killer on my hand, what the fuck are you trying to do to me? You know I have this Chavez case on my hands. This is a hobby for me — it gets me pussy, but it doesn't put money in my pockets like the Chavez case will." I stop here because this is the only man in the world who I know to shut up for because what's coming next is worse than anal probing a camel.

"You fuckin' slag! You owe this to the industry as well as your fans. Fuck law, you're richer than God already. Get your potatoes back in the sack and get to work on this book." His English accent overshadows the spit that enriches our conversation like too much wasabi on a fresh serving of unagi.

I take a red pen from a holder on his desk that says *Sync Inc.* and shove it in my pocket. The pen is worth a lot of money to a law student, but it is necessary to me because I can write novels only with these pens. I tell Nils I will do what I can and dial Ricardo's number to see how his Mexican *tres*-some went. I slump my way out of Nils's office because I know his eyes are on me, I can feel them on me like the glare of every woman I've just sodomized and treated to a load of —

"Hey, amigo, what's crackin'?" I spit the words at Ricardo through our digital connection, which transcends the boundaries of space and distance and me caring about Nils's eyes.

"Not so good, man, been lying here all day wondering why I can't fall in love no more."

"What the fuck is this drama? Did you call Lauren today?"

"No, man, no drama, but I couldn't stop thinkin' about how that brunette looked like Lauren. I kept calling her Lauren, calling out in the dark while she was trying to sleep with coke still on her ass…'Laaaauren, Laaaauren come rub me, baby. I will play your pussy like a flute.' I used to say that, and she loved it."

I wish I were there to cock punch this asshole.

"Sure, man, I will take you to the clinic to get checked out, no problem. You want an enema as well, or should I just pay a one-legged anything to fuck you? Play what? Like what? She laughed at that? Fuck me harder than Mona Lisa — "

"Fuuuck you, I can smell Marielle's influence like your latest favorite cum-flavoured salad that dresses your breath. I know she's the real reason you bailed last night."

"I got peed on this morning. Meet me at Stino's Dino in one hour, okay, chino?"

I hang up the phone, look in the mirror, and hate the fact that my face is once again making that same face it used to make when I was still capable of enduring pain.

CHAPTER ???

Stino's Dino is where all the trendy, out-of-work actors go to gossip about the shit that hasn't made the tabloid magazines yet. I've fucked eight out of the nine instructors from the yoga studio above it. The ninth is a guy named Mai from Singapore, and he would give his left nut (if he still had it) to fuck me or Ricardo. This is why we don't come here a whole lot, but the food is great and the service — well, the service is stellar on all fronts, if you catch my drift. I roll up into the lot and squeeze next to a famous someone's twenty-two-inch rims. I jump the door of my Lexus and stroll under the beaming silver arch that leads into Stino's.

The bouncer takes one look at me as I call him a useless piece of meat that I would eat if he were more tender and less of a faggot, and he gives a laugh, knowing that I will spend more here tonight than he will make in a week. I see Ricardo sitting at our regular spot with that swollen, half-hearted, pussy-eating smile he gets inside and out on his face.

"You smell like vag, amigo, and I know it isn't from the girl last night. This is the *I'm a bitch who sucks cock vag* that I smell, what the fuck is your problem, Dirty Sanchez?"

"Yo, man, no need for that shit, just feelin' down, that's all. Lauren left me a text last night while we were at the bar and I didn't want to tell you and ruin your night."

"Ruin my night? I was robbed in Santa Monica and woke up with piss nuts instead of Grape-Nuts for breakfast. What the fuck, man? Cut this shit, I can't believe you!"

"I know, amigo, it's not good and I know the rule…"

In unison, we both say, "No ducking the fuck, only fucking the cunty duck." What a love-enriched word.

At the same time, the family beside us, who are clearly on vacation from New Hampshire or Canada, give us an offended look and I can't hold back from spitting out, "You know what that means, kiddo?" It's a six-year-old kid sitting beside his dad with eager eyes, wondering if I'm some form of rock star. "It means you never bail on a lay, you stick them as hard as fuck until your cock runs empty like a camel that has run out of its hump juice in the middle of the desert. You never duck a good lay, and that includes thinking about ex-girlfriends before, after, or during sex."

The mother looks like she is going to tear my head off and shove it into the blender that is making my fruit smoothie. I give her a profile shot of my face, and she says to her husband, who has been staring at the tits on one of the yoga instructors in the next room and hasn't noticed a thing, that this is why they don't eat at trendy cafés that cost more than they make in a day. She is probably right, they shouldn't be eating here.

The waitress brings us our regular lunch with all the fixings we like. The meat is so tender that I wouldn't even trade it for a porn star's. The smoothie tastes better without my head in it. Many people would say that if my head were in it, it wouldn't fit the largest glass on the shelf; they are probably right.

"You know what we need to do, Ricardo?"

"What's that?" Ricardo says anxiously, yet he is obviously still preoccupied with the image of Lauren in his mouth.

"We need to ask a random girl in here the freakiest thing she would do with us and do it with her."

"What the fuck, man, you insa—?"

Before he can finish his sentence, I have already turned and asked the most beautiful girl in the place the question.

"Well, wouldn't you like to know," she responds.

"Yeah, I fuckin' would, that's why I asked. You're a living reason actions speak louder than words," I say with a smug grin on my face.

She clearly doesn't understand but realizes she might get to fuck two of the highest-rated celebrity lawyers on the West Coast, one of whom is also a famous writer, so she gives an awkward eye and says, "I know a place we can all have a threesome. One guy up the do-doop-de-do, one guy traditional, whatcha think?"

Ricardo is about to say something but I burst in and say, "An address would go really nice with this steak."

Now don't discredit me, I've eiffel towered my way from Paris to Porto to St. Petersburg and back with a skill that has ensured no other man's river of white has converged with my own, unless it's within her mouth — the fountain of youth, the history books of my life call it. Bring on the milk and cookies.

The girl's name is Daniela, and she reeks of gorgeous with a butterfly tattoo on her left shoulder that probably represents the freedom every girl says they have. To tell you the truth, I'm not fond of the idea of having my dick become a ben and jerrys special in one giant ice cream cone with Ricardo's cock, but I need to get Ricardo out of this rut because it's reflecting my own rut and my desire for Marielle. In awkward silence, we finish our meals and leave a large tip along with a hologram card of my cock that I'd had made for me when I met with the CEO of Topps, a playing card company in New York, over a legal consult. The whole deal was under the table, and it was to the surprise of a kid in Wichita, I believe, when my big old bat turned up instead of his Ken Griffy Jr. card. Beyond the matter, we leave the café and I tell Ricardo that he had better lose the earring because I will already feel gay enough being that close to him.

It's five o'clock and the sun is setting over LA, the land of opportunity. I don't know how American angels compare to other countries' angels, but from my experience in this city, the true angels of LA left long before it was built.

59

The apartment Daniela brings us to is quaint and reminds me of a place I once dreamt of living in back when I wore flannel shirts and torn jeans. She has been here before, the girl is well rehearsed. The room is prepped like a porn flick with red satin sheets, one big pillow in the shape of a heart in the middle of the bed, and a set of anal beads dangling from the lamp, which appeared to me to be a symbol for the fight Ricardo and I had about who would be stretching colon and who would be driving up the water hole — both of us jumping in the air at the beads for the rights over Gollum's cave.

"Hey, boys, looks like my dreams are about to come true: two men, one girl…who wants to moisten up my filthy little holes first?"

I win the debate over anal rights as I asked this chica to take a dip in the fountain of filth in the first place. She comes prancing in the room like a slutty school girl all dressed up for a Halloween party, a party offering multiple cream-stuffed ding dongs. I slowly tilt her over the bed and wink at Ricardo as I pour a drip of lube into her tight pink hole. She chirps that it's cold, but before she knows it I have my first two fingers grinding deep inside her. As if it is a cue, Ricardo strips down to his Mexican birthday suit and begins to penetrate her as she rides him and takes my fingers inside her. What happens next is something I have not experienced since grade school.

With no warning, the door breaks open with the force of a firecracker, and within seconds I am on the floor with my hands cuffed behind my head, dick sloppy but surprisingly harder than it had been before the insurgence. In a desperate attempt, I try to squeak out, "Pleaaaase, can I cum first?" but Daniela, the Mexican cockfighter, that sly bitch, kicks my cock like it is a rabid dog in Acapulco, turning my voluptuous member into a regressive school boy who has just been told that his new haircut makes him look like Ellen DeGeneres.

"What the shit!?" I yell, grasping my throbbing cock as one man drags an ATM machine out of a closet across the room from where I am rolling around like a pig in the mud.

Apparently, this particular senorita is wanted for the trafficking of cocaine and the theft of several ATM machines throughout the greater Los Angeles area. Luckily, one agent has a sense of humour, handing me his jacket and saying, "Well, Ayden Wallace, you sly dog, not enough business chasing celebs around, now you have to sleep with cocaine dealers. Hey…what the fuck is going on here, anyways?" He points to the anal beads, which are now strategically hanging above Ricardo's face as he lies on his back on the bed. The officer's plump, aged face turns from the brilliant shade of exhilaration it had been when he entered the room to a hue of pale embarrassment in less time than it would have taken me to make Daniela cum while giving her the Italian moose knuckle.

"Just a little fun and games is all," I say with a smug look beaming across my face. "This Mexican, though…I think he's illegal."

CHAPTER????

Every time I end up on the wrong side of the bars, I am slightly humbled. Sitting in a corner of the prison cell, the walls speak to me in the innocent foreign tongues of those who would have escaped these bars if they could have afforded, well, me. I sit here against a concrete wall realizing that in the grand scope and purpose that is life, I am a prostitute—a very, very expensive prostitute, up for hire at a premium only celebrities can afford.

"Wallace, your bail has been posted," an officer exclaims through the stale cell air. I walk through the steel doors with a 1980s western tune running through my head. This is why I love the law in America—justice is served simply because I have rich and powerful friends. I would feel guilt in actualization of this fact if it weren't for the black hole that was my childhood. The true justification allows the American dream to prevail, the promise of socioeconomic progression for those who possess the facets of successive Darwinian qualities. In this, I walk out of the correctional system unscathed—and slightly more popular—in the public eye.

The sun is exceedingly fresh after you have spent some time behind bars. As I walk into the space between the air, the sun's light flashes in my face and I see a glass room that appears to be my office, yet the company is different. The faces of geriatrics are around me, telling me I need to change, telling me stories of how their own fortune burned into misfortune. Airplanes fly past the windows, carrying faces from familiar places to unfamiliar destinations. There is a young man dressed in a tuxedo playing the piano, the ivory keys pulsing with a song I can taste in my ears but have a hard time comprehending where I know it from. I'm approached by a young woman who offers me ice cream with a vanilla smile. Her breasts spill out from her white blouse and into my face, yet I feel nothing. My arms are old, the skin spotted like the face of the sun, and I reach down and feel the plastic tubes that run into my arms, giving me the elixir of life, a pain killer that seems to hold at bay not only my central nervous system but my sex drive as well. I ask the lady in white to hold up a mirror; what I find is a man who looks like all men, no importance to his features, no handsome smile, no complexion, no real expression. I am a war veteran with the post-traumatic stress of a life lived vicariously through the foreign curves of too many girls and not enough women.

The man at the piano looks over and smiles at me. It's a real smile, a smile that relinquishes all judgement, bending itself in an upward motion for only one purpose: sympathy. In this, I cannot help to fight the warships that bombard my calloused heart with emotion. With this single lucid, unsettling moment, the salt that once made up my blood trickles down from my eye, covering the landscape that is my skin, weakened and scathed from the years wasted on not living and simply existing in a small hell that I have created within my own personal legend.

I come to and I feel the presence of warm concrete on my face. Not the cold, life-sucking concrete that pressed against my body moments ago behind bars, but a man-made earth that has been heated by the only thing natural in this city.

"Ayden!" I hear a voice through my left ear and feel the touch of a friend under my left arm. "You all right, amigo?"

Ricardo.

"Yeah, what happened? Where am I?" I say through the lapse of lucidity that I was experiencing.

"You must need something to eat, you came outside and just collapsed, down like a cheap—" I stop him and pat him on the back, feeling an expression of revelation and confusion over my face, body, and mind.

"All right, all right. Fuck. I'm fine, man, just get me home"

CHAPTER ?

If my pigmented parchment and white line-ingrained memory serve me correctly, there was a time and a place I lived on the fifth floor of a five-story building back in Victoria, a town barely labelled as a city on most maps of the world. The top floor of any building is always favoured over anything below, much like the social hierarchy every developing nation eventually subscribes to. On the top floor of a building in Victoria you don't hear the domestic disputes, the dogs barking to neglecting owners, the suction of lips on dicks, or the wail of an unhappy wife in what my gender studies textbook referred to as unconsensual sexual frustration and lamentation, a lamentation process that eventually occurs in all relationships. Some, mainly the world's enlightened polygamists, state that we all endure certain lamentation once we have had to embrace the fact that our maidens' vaginas, the ones we have sworn ourselves to, aren't a fee-free jizzum bank into which the male kind can deposit worthless loads of spunk whenever and wherever.

It was on this fifth floor in a stucco-encrusted building that aged the entire neighbourhood back to the 1970s where I discovered that my gender studies class really needed to re-evaluate its syllabus and reconsider the need to push males from their male hegemony into the rants and enlightened paradigm shifts of neo-feminist movements. Sometimes, as most polygamists would agree, men are from vaginas and women are from vaginas — that's a lot of points on the board for the vagina; let's appreciate it to the fullest and penetrate as many as humanly possible.

I attempted to claim recuse on the grounds of my internal conflict between banging the odd girl on the weekend and the writing I was doing in my gender studies classes. I excused myself from my writing and led myself into the faculty of vagina studies in my fifth-floor penthouse, an apartment that required water maintenance every fucking week, which meant saving jugs of water in the fridge on a regular basis for post-sex hydration purposes. Throughout the course of said water outages, I routinely considered dating women who had just given birth in order to maintain a healthy intake of fluids from their tits.

This is Ayden Wallace learning that defiance leads one from the Left, way, way, fucking way to the Right. I don't currently seek out breasticles to suckle on for nutrients — but then again I still do suck on them for a different form of survival, and then again, I currently can afford my own stock of Fijian-flavoured water. Maybe I haven't changed, but for the photo album I hope to someday show someone of meaning to me, I won't take any photos. I'm never taking photos, not of stucco buildings or of the progression or lack thereof in my life. If I could have heard the man on the second floor yelling his better half into a nightmare that she wished she had only heard about in a case study in a gender studies class, I would have realized how unlucky every human truly is who lives an ignorant life on the fifth floor of a five-story building. My ignorance perpetuated as I rose up to find myself in LA on the eighty-eighth floor of an eighty-seven floor building.

I made a game of influencing people's lives down on the streets from my fifth-floor abode. I would hear couples arguing about aggressive smiles in bars, about the looks, sucks, and jerks from foreign individuals that had occurred throughout their war of the night. I would hear life stories of men sick and tired of paying gratuitous amounts of money for wine that would only spill faster and faster from the tip of their deflated shitake mushroom heads the more they drank; a sad reminder of the price of the actual mushrooms that were added to the food they had ordered. An addition to the bill that would foster future destitution and a certain dissolve in male sexual functioning.

I had heard it all—the missteps in life and the prostitutes who constantly offered to provide an in-the-moment reprieve from oncoming sexual dysfunction. If I had learned anything from my mother, I think it was that one should never judge another who is embracing the moment. This is why I left the prostitutes alone and targeted my efforts at change on the other passersby who could still benefit from my drunken cries: "Hey, sweetheart, a blow job goes a long way to restore that smile," and "Hey! Hey! I bet his cock tastes better when dipped in peach apple sauce, it's cheaper than dinner tonight, you should try it now!" A childish game not unlike Go Fish.

I had often hoped that my existential interventions, bellowed from the fifth-floor penthouse that I couldn't then afford but could definitely own today, provided some positive result. When speaking of today and my disorientation, I wish that I were back in the moment with those couples. Old holy gods may have preached righteousness, but the sins of today they could never have fathomed even in the darkest of times. Playing god on my fifth-story balcony, I discovered the celebrity within. To mitigate my desire to protect the unfortunate, I began to defend those gods on fifth-story penthouses. The limbs of trees are built up not on the foundations of something different and greater than themselves — the marginalized provide services for the marginalized and perpetuate their need to exist and acquire, albeit small, capital gains. A marginalized individual keeps another in business the same as a celebrity lawyer in LA keeps a misguided, sad, depressed, and alcoholic someone in the business of life-sucking, shitty social modelling. That stucco building seems oddly familiar, yet this current state of ruthless being is always growing, and apparently not even the rude confines of imprisonment can turn my eyes from the impure white that fills the air of every room I enter. I think back to Victoria, I think outside of where I should have been all my life. I'm always away on some island and never in the moment. Maybe this makes my writing, but then again, maybe this foreshadows certain regret. Ask the couples on the street, maybe they will know.

CHAPTER ???

Over the next few months, my sex drive dwindles with every strenuous court case and every failed attempt I make to compile some sort of novel. Introspection is taking hold, and I am becoming a silent writer and lover. In all respects, I have become an alcoholic ghost of the day, drifting from one shallow experience to the next. Call it depression, but there is a story in this that I am hoping will soon flourish like the magic that is spring. It isn't Marielle, it's this fascination with a dream, that dream of the piano man's smile, my attraction to that lady in white I didn't want to sleep with but wanted to learn more about. In Ricardo's words, I was a giant *coño*, but in my own, I am becoming more lost in something unfamiliar and important by the minute. With every passing airplane overhead, I am beginning to find hope in the things that I once regretted. A part of me wants some finality to my story, to this story that is being told over and over like a record on repeat. Existentially speaking, I secretly wish someone would press the fast-forward button on my future steps in life, allowing me to see where I will finally be hanging up my Italian-made shoes. I am hoping for someone to yell at me from atop a stucco building on the fifth floor and tell me what the fuck to do with my coño and life.

But the piano has stopped, and the room has gone from containing brilliant shining air to a white cloud of unknown. I have stepped out of my comfortable fuck-and-flee routine and have plunged headfirst into what feels like an omniscient state of being, a state in which I am watching my life unfold within a sharing circle of individuals aged beyond the years they should have lived and who have stories as poisoned as those of my own.

The largest plague of all has arrived in the city of Diablos; it is a life-shattering illness and a god-like presence that has given way to the feeling of a bottomless ocean. That rainbow of my life is now dipping itself into my memories, and just as I am expecting a shit-coloured skyline above me, I see only white.

Records of our lives provide flavour through alcoholic consumption, the lubricant to the wheels that turn the tapes of our lives against the silk screens of the world, assuming that we put to parchment while we're still under its influence. Hello, Hollywood, I've met you now, I wish I could respond in a mature matter of fact way, but alcohol has always done more than lubricate this vulgar tongue of mine. It's more than K-Y Jelly for the words in my head, which spill out against dry paper in the form of Hollywood Cockufornian scripts. Scripts read into the pulsing, conflict-loving ears of the Americas and beyond. I am writing again, or at least trying.

I sit down in the sand and begin to scribble out a screenplay about a girl who turned her back on a man when he leaves for islands far away instead of heading to a war in some conflict zone. Possibly a World War II write — no that's been done, so I begin to sketch out my own apocalyptic war zone with all the blood, piss, and shit that sputters out from the gutters of LA and into the ocean. Hmm, I suppose I'm a large addition to the shit in the sea, knowing that back in Victoria, where the oceans are protected from such filth, I once was an advocate for removing it. Victoria, the land of prosperity. Maybe my leading protagonist, my hero of the West, my Mr. Manifest Destiny, will be from a nice town like Victoria or some Northern state along the West Coast. Maybe he will collect photos from his travels and mail them back to his maiden on the mainland from his harboured boat, or a maybe it's a wreck in Samoa or Fiji. Or maybe he won't send any letters and photos at all. Maybe he will begin to suffocate on his regrets and jump into a sea of plastic and shit and become smothered by the world's lack of environmental foresight. I think this book would look good on the stands at LAX — which means I have to think of something more graphic and edgy. Something that will exclude itself from the shitty stockpile of sociopsycho babble that is thrown together every year and offers no real solution to the world's social anxiety or the inability of nations and humans alike to make real friends with one another.

Classic chapter one, Social Psychology 101, gin and tonic–infused first-year undergraduate student self-penile promotion material; the worst in the current world of LAX publications and bestsellers. I begin to write about surfing, but the pen trembles and I can't find hope in it anymore. I begin to write about Nils, that classic assfucker from England, and become too frustrated to continue.

I stand up, admiring the outline of a shallow figure that my body has forged in the sand, and begin to walk down the beach as I sip on a bottle of gin and suck on the exhaust pipe of my favourite relaxation agent. Bonfires begin to illuminate the beach despite the signs every quarter mile outlawing this course of recreation. There are no signs prohibiting drugs and alcohol, so I continue down the beach, attempting to put together a string of words worthy of presenting to Nils and the world. Well, it's not as if signs would stop me anyway. I'm always missing the signs, it seems, and not just the ones that encourage my growth as a moral human being but also the ones that may someday lead me to something, anything, worthy of living out a meaningful life and dying in a nice retirement home.

CHAPTER ??

Home becomes a relative place after the release of my novel *Blessed Love*, which "brilliantly portrays the comings and goings of a heart strewn up on the fine wires of Californian complacency and ill-mannered recklessness" — whatever the fuck that means. I walk down the streets of New York City, Seattle, Portland, Toronto, Miami, and every other city worth mentioning in the united front of unemployment and war mongering. I tire of the political promise in the news of a better-educated, better-prepared, and better-applied future. My face begins to show the lines of a political science writer who has just come to realize that no matter what he has to say, the world does the opposite in its own self-imposed, devastating delight. Everywhere my feet travel, they are heavy.

It's three o'clock in the morning and I'm standing in SFO with a leather shoulder bag and a pocket full of condoms and lube — my usual travel care package. I gaze across the hall at the moving walkway we humans use to keep from exercising our lazy asses in this obese, over-saturated country. I see a woman and her obese child huffing and puffing for air as they travel down the magic carpet. What the fuck.

"Hey, take your kid on a walk, Rosie," I say and point to the television screen that is airing a presidential speech about enlightening our kids on the mistakes we have made both politically and personally over the last century.

"Why don't you mind your own fucking business, you fucking cunt," she wails back as she drifts by on Aladdin's magic carpet of trans and saturated fat.

"The fat lady has sung! Just preaching the words of the future, ma'am, don't let your coronary be his too." I laugh loudly at the moment of humour I have made for my surrounding travel partners.

Losing interest in the interaction as the opera singer drifts away into a life of anger, I notice a cute, tight brunette giggling to herself at the situation that is my life. She is seated next to two large men, looking desperate for a move in any direction away from them.

"You know what really bothers me, though?" I say in her direction with my eyes, body, and mouth. "The fact that we can elect a women president, but we cannot take the goddamn armrests off airport seats so that someone can catch a decent fucking sleep between flights." Not to my surprise, with a wave of brunette sunlight, she tosses her hair behind her shoulders, picks up her Louis Vuitton bag, and struts over to me with a swagger that could make any cocaine cowboy keel over and die.

"Hi," I say. "I'm hard and bored, what's your name?" I speak with hard confidence in light of her amusement with my sixth grade–inspired fat jokes and recent literary success.

"Wet and barely legal," she replies.

"Walking to the handicapped washroom."

"Following with sex toys in my bag."

"Interested and feeling slightly in the mood to humiliate."

"Tight and ready to comply," she moans, rolling her eyes with the intent of erotic foreshadow.

In the midst of our verbal fucking, I slide my fingers up her tight black skirt and into her warm slit. Feeling around, ignoring the faces and eyes burning at us, I feel something hard about two centimetres south. She notices and holds my head up with two of her fingers under my chin, speaking gently into my ear. "I've had that plug in my ass all my life, just waiting for a cock like yours to replace it."

In this moment of pure, unadulterated honesty, I push and pull the butt plug like the on-and-off switch of a carousel made of bumping dildos, causing her to moan with an intensity that even I feel requires some place more private to contain.

Moving across the marble airport floor like some sort of erotic, east Maldivian dance, the *So You Think You Can Dance* crowd applauds on the inside for my ability to not give a shit. With one last waltz, we kick the handicapped bathroom door open and I slam her hard against the 1960s tile wall. She has an honest sexuality about her, her skin secreting the smell of oranges and mangoes, freshly picked on a spring morning, and the light of the room gives way to all the dark places she has wanted to go for so long.

Making my way down the curves of her Beverly Hills–toned body, I hold her up against the wall with my arms above my head, like the great god Atlas holding everything that is this hazy noire earth. With half my strength devoted to holding my filthy world up against the wall and half devoted to sucking on its tight button, I lap in her juices, taking a large bite out of her mango and allowing the nectar to cover me like a frostbitten tourist tasting tropical fruit, fresh from the vine, for the first time.

She moans louder than a thousand jet engines and tastes as sweet as she smells. I know from experience that this is not always the case; I've sometimes ducked down into the wet chasms of a woman only to find a cave covered in thick vines and moss. With this thought, I relinquish my duties as Atlas, the primordial Titan, and take up the throne of Himeros, longing for the tip of my sword to stroke between the warm enclosure that is the entrance to her soul.

BANG! A loud knock on the door that certainly does not sound like the polite warning a flight attendant often gives when I'm balls deep, 20,000-feet above the Pacific, interrupts. I lock eyes with the current goddess of my life, and with a flutter of her eyes and a strong grasp on my back, I enter her and start to push myself deep past the boundaries of giving a fuck. The banging on the door gets louder as her screams echo against its thunderous displeasure with our public display of fucking all worldly values. These Mission: Impossibles keep me alive. What they really need on the other side of this door is a taste of this mango. With this thought, her insides tighten around my cock, attempting to draw my soul from my body. This isn't going to cut it, I need more.

I open the door with my right hand and grab a small, amateur-looking security guard by the shirt collar and pull her inside the washroom that has now become our Garden of post-sin Eden, the part they left out of the Bible. As the sound of skin-on-skin pounding continues, I look at the twenty-some-year-old security guard and use my eyes to say, *Listen, you may lose your job, but this is a goddamn ever-after fairy tale. Drop your uniform and values at the door, sweetheart.*

As if taken by my thoughts and the sexual energy in the room, the young, athletic-looking security guard drops her job title and pleated pants to the floor in one fluent movement. As if it were rehearsed in the dated instructional video she was privy to in her training on what to do if confronted by Ayden Wallace and a risky situation, she sticks four fingers knuckles deep into her own water party.

"Jesus Christ." I smile; the world has a goddamn action plan for me. Before I can say *good girl*, she is on all fours, sucking my balls like a hungry piranha in the middle of the West Amazon. Her grasp is cold, like the confines of handcuffs, but her touch is as soft as a grandmother's heart. I begin to feel her tongue travel up my shaft, lapping in the juices of my pre-flight mistress.

BANG! A new knock intrudes on the latest travelling sex show of my life; the intensity of our world together grows.

With the security guard's legs wrapped around my goddess's head, I continue to thrust into her as all three of us begin to gyrate like the pictures on a wall at the beginning of an earthquake. The banging on the door turns into slamming, each slam resembling the disheartening reminder that Western morals are slowly working their way back into the room. In fighting this, as I've done my whole life, I pull the girls' hair back with both my hands, like a gaucho grabbing the manes of two wild stallions. With one giant groupgasm, there is an explosion of cum and sweat as all three of us fall to the floor in total exhaustion, smiles as wide as a Moroccan merchant's.

With a deep laugh, the party comes to an end as the door crashes open with all the fury and anger that exists in this moral-laden world. All three of us are immediately placed in the cold grasps of reality and the bindings of California State law. I recall that prison is a place I have recently been but maintain my composure, knowing that it is more likely this incident will make *Time* magazine than that I will go back behind bars. I smile with a lady-juice-drenched grin:

"Ladies, it's been a pleasure."

CHAPTER ??

What kind of story do you tell when a love story just won't do? Is there a genre for the fucked-up lives that burn under the Californian sun like ripe tomatoes shrivelled up to the lengths of ancient mummy cock? What sort of man creates a world where such a question need be asked? It has been four months since I was given the right to pass back into my home from the cold confines of immigration; I paddle out into the fog of work, dodging my boss and the shitty coffee, which is the perfect mix of laxative and spice in the morning. Days continue as days do, though in the spirit of progress they drift for others and not for me.

Every word I write deteriorates into some self-loathing short story about how much I miss Marielle, a girl who left my physical self ten years ago. Stories of revelation, stories of this world that elicit such hate in me, a bipolar opposition to the sanity everyone wants to possess. I wrote such gold only a year ago, gold that has transgressed into many more invigorating experiences in airport washrooms with scantily dressed females. But the gold is starting to tarnish beyond the polishing abilities of tongue lubricants and bong hits.

Where does a man go when the oak church doors' hinges are welded shut by the choices he has made? When the ocean is a frozen tundra of memories that cannot be broken open and offer no refuge to one's soul. When the clouds above cut the sunlight in and out of your face as you sweat your life away in your Hugo Boss suit on Sunset Boulevard—nose outstretched, a fiend for the closest dose of white powder, unable to touch the view of a skyline or hear the music of the Whiskey. Where does a man go when he writes the words he can't say, when he borrows lines from those who borrowed time from the greats of old? We are a walking generation of recycled air and word pollution, spitting out defamations of ten minutes ago and how far behind we are to the now. So ignorant and full of some bliss forged from the darkest chasms of loneliness, sitting in our leather armchairs made by the hands of the poor, the enlightened, the realists in some faraway land.

We are always looking for that one sycamore to awaken our feminine intuitions and deliver gifts of great knowledge—fruit-bearing knowledge that supersedes our own personal self-interest. We delve deeper into our own garbage and fail to actualize some form of empathetic wisdom for the world that suffers around us. I'm a man of few principles, a man who has done little with the air placed in my labile lungs. Lethargic, I travel like a rough-furred goat from field to field in the North African plains of raw, unforgiving, inorganic dirt—dirt I knowingly sucked the life from with every dick-in-the mud moment of

80

my personal journey. I fervently contemplate the darkest of my days as I sit against the only altar that will stand to hear my words. Atop the roof of my cubicle, overlooking the angels of lost, I collapse with my hands pressed against my face, the never-ending black water of my existence spilling out onto the roof beneath me, evaporating into the sky instantaneously as tears touch the dark tar that is my soul. This isn't the worst nightmare a man can have, but it's enough.

Where does a man go when no one will have his prayer? Where does a man go when he has left himself? Where does a man go when no world fits his own?

CHAPTER ????

The whiskey glass is half-full, contrary to the way I'd been feeling just days ago about the world's moral and ethical decision to keep me alive and thriving off the finest labium a Cockufornian's lips can find. I like alliteration, especially when I'm encasing my rhymes inside the pink libations of female cum. If you've ever tried to sing a Queen song with your mouth full of pink, you catch my vibe. I am frothing at the thought of a glass that is half-full, and I know I am a cheesy motherfucker for doing it. But sometimes we are all that cheesy motherfucker, just waiting to be taken home.

The canyons along the Californian highway open up like the legs of an unfamiliar woman, legs I'd been trying to sink my entire soul into for some time now. There is something about leaving the entire world you know behind, even if it's one filled with every vice that keeps the suit on your back and your dick out of the sand and inside the juice. I'm wearing an Indonesian bintang singlet, stained with the sweat I had spilt across the world while on surf trips that created a space within me; the space that was driving my cockmobile further and further into the Californian blue, leaving the blackness of love behind in the city of perdition.

The road wound like the coming days for a newly crowned king, the sun spilling across it with the elegance of the brightest fire's shadow. I reflected and related myself to the oncoming blackened earth, manufactured fingerprints of our progress stretched out in front of my soul, guiding me swiftly towards a point I hadn't visited in years, a literal and internal point that would soon either devastate or release me from my servitude. These times burn in such devious ways that even flames become confused and lost in the rhythm of the wind. I speed along the freeway, glass half-full and mind slowly becoming half-empty; I would soon be found in a city my heart would call home.

Oregon, my destination, stretches like forever over a land covered in a purity that cannot have been made by man. I pull over at a store just before the California state border and check in with the same twenty-year-old I had met six hours earlier in Eureka.

"Fifty-six doll-ers, man," the clerk postures as he checks out my status in contrast to my shirt. "You have kids, man?"

"What makes you think I'm a man to have a family, kid," I say, genuinely interested and terrified at the same time.

"That's Indo beer, bro, you don't strike me as the surf type, more like LA highbrow fuckin' OC shit, makin' bank and all, hey? What are you, a lawyer or something? Big break from the workweek or what?"

"Something like that…bro." I gather my change into the fist of a teenager in angst and storm past the shit-stained walls that encase the store, tail between my legs and my humility puncturing my skin like a serrated knife crossing the borders of someone's fragile personality. Threatened, I pull over into the first cheap hotel I can find, hoping that the walls of poverty surrounding my body and mind tonight will be enough to bring back some form of Marielle and the guy within me who could call another guy *bro* without insinuating insult. I missed me.

I take the man's awkward eye at the motel's front desk as a compliment to the fact that the LA shell is slowly shedding off my identity. I seriously consider setting fire to my Lexus and pissing on the ashes but decide to drive ten minutes up the road and buy a flask of Sailor Jerry, the only lifelong lover I've ever had, and sit on the fringe of what matters at the lines drawn by the ocean. Her personality is inviting; with the smooth candour of promise, she invites my legs into her like a woman inviting another life to grow inside her. My phone rings. It's Ricardo's grin staring back at me through LED light waves, waves that make me smash the image out of my retinas with one swift throw. He's just trying to be my friend, but the only real one I have tastes better and has more spice. I sip more rum and cough at the displeasure it creates at the back of my throat.

I don't pass out like the times before when my body was more death than life. I wade in the warmth and cold of my peace as the tension in my eyes, face, and roots begins to fill with humility and the world I should be grateful to live in. I pull the flask of spiced Island rain into my lips and pace my thoughts with the silence of Jesus's last supper. Down the beach, a fiery beacon burns and I can hear the echo of free spirits as a guitar sings their lives into a swirl of playful blue and white flames. The funny thing about fire is that from close up it speaks of comfort, safety, and calm, but from afar its shadows offer no asylum from the darkness of the heart — it's shadows dance off the surroundings as though our egos are forcing the world to stay away, out of our lives, as if to say that the unknown is a threat against our autonomy and self. Nothing could be further from the truth. I've become used to the shadows of flames, to lying on the fringes of flames. I've come to learn how to embrace the change shadows create and how to move between them like enlightened castaway angels. The morning star, a name given to both Jesus and the fallen angel of the underworld, I bounce like a spark of light between the shadows of their flames, rising on one side and falling hard on the other. The battle is half-empty and my warriors are still parched.

The music down the beach continues as I take to my feet and begin a sailor's march across the rocks that have been beaten into something softer. I think for a second that we are all the same: once hardened, now soft.

The moon projects itself over the islands out at sea like a drive-in movie. The sailors of SoCal are happy tonight as the wind whisks them away into the dreams they are already living.

I shake hands with the night and retire to my motel room with a good start on my hangover and a strong finish to the emptiness that led me here. We

who enter LA never leave the same. And we who
retire on the beach with money but no appreciation
for the importance of not having it are amiss
altogether.

CHAPTER ??

The morning is strong, its light breaking the rusted window of the motel room and shattering the yellowed walls back into a brilliant white. I roll over and look at the floor. I see my suit and I see my shorts, both cast out on the ground: a clear choice to be made. I grab my shorts and singlet and bask in the steam of the shower as it cascades hard hot water across my manicured body. I think for a second that I should turn and head back home, that I've found my night of peace between the shadows and am ready to tell the story of my softer side to my next lover.

I flick on the TV and watch a story of a missing boy on the local Northern California news, personalizing it for a second before realizing that there really is a boy without a family today. This isn't LA, this is a place where one person on the news makes sense and matters. Say what you will about a white-picket fence and a familiar vagina that gets tired and old, but if something goes wrong, your neighbours and their deteriorating love for their wives' vaginas will be with you until the end. This is something I can't say I've found in the cycle of my life for some years.

I walk out the motel door, leaving my seven-thousand-dollar suit on the floor with a note that reads, *I wish this attire on no one in this place.*

My tires barely begin to warm from the friction of the road when I notice a familiar sight from my youth. I pull over, creating a dust storm that would anger drivers in these parts, and park next to a diner I once stole from when I was surfing just north of here, surviving off the land and the angst to leave my hometown, which pushed me further and further in a direction I often feel I should have continued on.

"Hello, good day, how are you doing today?" Her voice has a slightly southern hint to it, and southern hospitality is exactly what I need.

"Hey, place looks good, it's been a while since I've stopped in these parts," I say in a voice lacking the familiar dickbag tone I had perfected over the years.

"Oh yes, yes! Old Wilkes came back from his time in the big city with a bucketload of money and put it all to good use in rebuilding this fine community—"

"Sorry," I interject with a bit of dickbagness. "What is the name of this town again? I always used to stop through, but, uh, yeah, young days are a bit of a daze and I missed the sign on my way in."

"Oh sir, no need to apologize, we here are in the township of Cambria, California, home of the Hearst Castle itself." Her pride is refreshing, and her eyes are honest in their refusal to judge as they graze over my face. I want to create love with her, I do.

"This here was the first gas station in all of Cambria, these stone walls have been here since its inception, there's lots of great stories held tightly between these stones, stories from travellers and blue collar workers like myself. And don't let me forget to mention the secrets, oh dear landy, there's secrets in these walls and boy do they ever speak of life as it once was. Real secrets, the ones people search far and wide for in them big sky-scraped type things. You know, I am from a large city in the south, but once I found these stone walls, well, God bless my heart I'd say that I found home."

Her honest way of living is enough to bring the heavens down in my sunken eyes. Her hair is twisted strawberry blonde taffy and her face, aged with wrinkles, forms around her smile rather than her cocaine and alcohol addiction. The soft ocean breeze and piano music fill the air, lending to some form of visual symphony — a photo, a painting of where it all began and where I can only hope to end. She is Marielle, embraced within the confines of a moment in the Northern California sun as it splits itself between the cracked panes of glass, which gives this moment more character than an architect could ever dream of artificially encapsulating in a structure. As she turns to pour a glass of water for the table next to mine, Cambria brings me to my knees and my legend changes.

"Oh sir, I'm so incredibly sorry, did I say something? Oh, here's a napkin, don't feel the need to stop, but if you, if you need something for your face, I'm so sorry —"

"No, no, it's fine, I just, you remind me of a loved one and this place is just — Sorry, I have to go." I rise from my chair as if Lucifer has been given passage back to heaven and leave my table surrounded by memories and stone to join in on the parade that is the present, the here, the now.

I kick my feet out the door and begin to run past my Lexus, past the sex, drugs, and litigation, and down to the closest surf shop. My feet are beating with blood and I find myself at the door of something I have longed to keep closed. I hit the water, the salt spraying up in my face like a skydiver piercing a loaded cloud. I paddle hard, get smashed continually for a set or two, and before I know it I am sitting outside of the reef; outside of myself.

The ocean is pulsating and breathing, moving and drifting over my skin, absorbing me into the depths of an ambiguous reality; one choice would find me learning and hurting, one would find me kissing Marielle. Every wave brings me closer to her and every wave brings me farther away and into something new. As the sun sets on my lactic muscles and aging smile, I begin to recognize a legend formulated out of the reality that my heart has not swallowed itself in drugs and pussy in fear of never seeing Marielle but rather in fear of not coming back to this. My addiction is a blackened forest that transgresses into a downward spiral further and further away from this. I want to be the next Wilkes of some hidden community on the coastline of nowhere.

And as my story ends I post this image on the biography of my life, an image that sees me leaving the unnatural giants of the sky for trees and the living energy that thrives in the company of all else that is living. I leave my life with an epiphany that brings me back to grade school, back to where I first learned to write of how I felt about the girl in the third row. Where writing should have taken me and where I should have looked instead of grasping at the dark hues of the California celebrity underbelly that forged my litigation methods. I leave now with the promise of something far beyond my frustration that you will never know or feel this moment until you experience it. My epiphany transcends the words of prophets, for prophets can only offer words and never the experience. Tell me a story, but never forget to leave out the ending. Take my hand and leave it, for I will never find the notes within the music while you're holding it.

I am back in white, and I wonder, I do, if this is real or if this is someone else's. I hear the piano — a song that has been tailoring my steps like an antiquated existential overture — but this is not the beginning, it is the end.

PART II

CHAPTER ?

I sit here in the middle of this lonely corridor surrounded by metallic birds that glisten with that same arrogance humans portray when they think they have conquered and replicated yet another facet of what nature does so perfectly. The glass walls have a silver trim, which offers warmth and comfort to the lone traveller who waits companionless, lacking the real warmth of conversation. Although music often serves as my companion, the music here is ear wrenching, that classic '80s rock you pray in every religious tongue had never been written. I would expect a classical symphony, but this? This is utter shit. I open up a surf magazine I had purchased from an ill-faced woman at the duty-free magazine shop. She appeared to have once made her living supplying travellers in Thailand with services only spoken of in gender studies classes in college and to now provide libations at low international prices to those same people across the taboo barriers of the Pacific in her current profession.

Along the same line of work, hauling luggage carts that hold people's small tokens of familiarity from airplane to airplane is one of the most important jobs here, ensuring that certain catastrophe doesn't arise and leave people stranded material-less in small Australian towns. What is purgatory if not a place where the materials we own leave us out to dry if one asshole doesn't do his job right? I think for a moment that this is surely some cacophony that I've heard in some shitty neo-liberal movie on some flight to shitty North American somewhere.

The city in the distance ignites from the blistering sun, and through the haze of human existence, buildings stand like giants marching on a warpath, shouting cries of some subliminal finality with no regard for the lives of men who are trying to leave the bloody battle of capitalist fundamentalism behind. It's a long battle, a mental and physical battle that requires one to forego a fight with the superego. A superego that is the desire to live in a box with four decorated walls strewn with images of classic musicians who dared to push past the nine-to-five and into something more surreal: simple, safe, secure, and certain death at the age of twenty-five. The id, on the other hand, is what I'm about to step into. Something impulsive, something lacking the certain intrinsic common drive that most humans possess to live in congregations of large, towering pillars lined with populated and overpriced streetcars. If I were so bold as to ask what is ego, I think I would find that the inside of a metallic bird to Mexico once a year would suffice as a mind-soothing remedy for most of the internal crises humans face while living in the "super" ego. That shit isn't so super if you ask me. I worry about what I'll mean by this when it's all over, I wonder why I'm concerned with psychology, and if Freud used cocaine, why the fuck can't the rest of us?

The smell of jet fuel brands my senses and reminds me that the grey light on the red horizon feels sorry for me but does not wish me to be here any longer. I lock myself into the cold fact that if I could fly this plane, I would fly it into the sun. I hope, to attain suicidal bliss, that the pilot has the same charts as me, for it would be a shame to end up anywhere else but a fire-enshrined Hieronymus Bosche portrait of some hell right now. The smell is growing stronger as the room begins to fill up with other humans — humans with broken hearts, bathing suits, smiles on their faces, worries in their minds, and hope in their luggage, which they watch from the window as it passes by on a trolley. This *is* purgatory, this is a place where we humans have the opportunity to change, or to embrace ourselves for who we are, or to indulge ourselves in the plastic ideology of the great Western compromise.

I arrived at LAX early in the morning, departing from the total destruction that was my past, a past that existed only moments ago and now seems like a lifetime far gone, left inside the diminishing photos in some album. When you step through customs into an intercontinental dream, it has a way of devouring your pain and giving you hope. The hope of something new, something exciting, and something worth writing home about — if you still have a home to write to.

As a child, the one thing I really enjoyed about travelling was the intercom; don't ask me why, but every time I heard a Spanish woman speak over an intercom it reminded me that I was going to be moving somewhere and embarking on some sort of an exploration. It wasn't until recently that I discovered that these journeys were never about where my physical self was going but rather about which direction my mind was growing. That French woman played more of a role in my life, over that crackling intercom, than any other person I care to think of. She was the voice of reason, and the voice of change. "Welcome aboard Flight 726, bound for introspective discovery." I love that woman, and I would spend my life, my dying days, beside her if she weren't but a reminder to me that I was once in love with something real, something tangible and remote to the dreams of being away from the factual and the haptic, driven needs of being a human in this world. The French woman is once again speaking to me, telling me she knows why I'm here, what I'm doing, and where I'm going. I find faith in this, though I never know whether I can trust her; the same goes for loving a real human, I guess.

The crowds are thickening now. I look across the terminal to the sun, which is turning from grey to a deep green, and my eyes transition in the same manner as I see a young couple holding hands, excited to spend a holiday together in whatever paradise they believe fit. I hope they discover someday what I have: that paradise can't be purchased over the Internet or at a ticket counter, no matter how many stars a resort has to its name. I don't mean to sound omniscient and enlightened — okay, senile — but there is something, some bitterness that gives way to intellect for me. I guess anyone who allows the unknown to protect them from what they know deserves respect in my eyes. Allowing what you know to protect you from the unknown is a very dark path to go down. I think most people who live in this way die looking through windows at metallic birds in the sky, wondering what life would have been like if they had embraced the fact that humans can fly, the fact that the unknown has a lot more to offer you than what you already know.

"Flight 482 with service to Honolulu is now boarding passengers in rows eighteen through thirty-two. Please have your passport open to your photo. Aloha, everybody!"

The hordes pile up, giddy with pleasure that they are about to board a momentary release from the superego, delving into the old savings account for a quick refresher from the mainland's massacre of their relationships' love languages. I wait in silence as the dollar leis and the aloha shirts file one by one down the corridor of the only office a pilot ever knows. I look up into the tired eyes of the service clerk, who looks as displeased with the masses as I feel. We acknowledge each other's inability to cope with the drowning of our own happiness, and I pass down the terminal and towards seat C, row 24.

I entertain the perfectly choreographed dance of negotiating my shit with someone else's shit in the overhead compartment. I've stuffed my blue Adidas duffle bag with my only remaining belongings: a compass, a container of surf wax, a porn magazine, some board shorts, a few singlets, a pair of sandals, and a hopeful wad of American bills. They squish into a pale woman's bronze Lois Vuitton bag, offering an ironic look into where I could have gone and where I am going. The facial expression she throws in my direction deteriorates the confidence I once had in leaving behind my unit in a pillar of concrete comfort. I cast my gaze down at the same old purple-patterned, fart-encrusted airplane seat that is to carry me to a more real form of prosperity. I snap my seat belt into place and ignore the safety video, which allows me to notice a set of eyes tracing their gaze my way as the plane pushes into thinner oxygen levels above cloud cover.

"Hey, man" — the guy looks into my lap at my open surf magazine — "you surf or what?" He asks me this with a slight hint of *I'm only asking because I want everyone on this plane to know that I surf, that I'm cool.*

I respond with an equally histrionic phrase, one that is used in the surfing world by those who consider themselves humbled. "Yeah, I did a bit of it back in my day." I look around to see who is watching and hope that it's the girl holding hands with her boyfriend.

With surfers, there is always the chase for the perfect wave, yet we all know that this is insatiable, so we continue to compare our idea of the perfect wave with that of every other surfer we meet. It's the perfect cockfight in Thailand and the perfect measuring stick for any man's shaft.

"Ha! You sound like my old man, brah, we're the same age, don't pretend you're the brodhisattva, man…I've met guys like you, I know your type, brah. Ha!"

There is some truth in this; I am being the standoffish douche bag who, I have so often reiterated, ruins the sport for me, and he has caught me: the master of surf Zen has now turned into an agro old fuckwad.

"You know how it goes, man, we're all that type at one point or another, especially when we're confronted about something we all want to brag about." I'm truly a Zen con artist.

"Ha! True enough, brah! Where you headed? Waikiki? This ticket here is a one-way back to O'ahu, straight up North Shore bound — Rockies, Pipe, Gas Chambers, V-land. So what's your deal? Where you staying?"

"Ah, I'm headed to Kailua-Kona once we land in Hono," I say with obvious hesitancy, knowing the job I have lined up there means I will be sacrificing some major surf time on the North Shore.

"No way, you staying in O'ahu, man, you surf for real? You staying with me, man, I'll hook you up — low budget, no problem. I know of this cherry campsite right in Malaekahana, fifteen minutes from Pipe, brah, shoots, no worries, yeah, you'll like Malaekahana — real locals, brah, hospitality, we go, we go."

Despite all the times I have embraced a change in plans — well, at least before I had met her — I feel compelled to decline the invitation like turning down standard imagery in a lonely department store: an easy decision that is dry and covered in dust. There is so much uncertainty in my life that a promised job in Kailua-Kona seems to offer at least some form of stability for me; it is my rock on a seafloor made of slippery memories, and even if that rock is a fruit-picking job on a farm full of coconut-juice-covered hippies, it is certainty.

"I, uh, I dunno, I've got plans," I say, knowing that I have become transparent, especially in my intention to remain grounded in the false reality that life is better when you reject the certain impermanent condition of this world. I wish I never bought that magazine.

"Shoots, we go, we go, brah, it's no worries, live the aloha, what's your name?"

CHAPTER ???

Johnny, Hawai'ian born and raised on the North Shore, is a local who carries on the vibe of the Aloha Spirit. Anything you want on the island of O'ahu, this guy can find it. The truth of the matter is that even though I am scared shitless of the unknown, I have heard my Spanish mistress on the intercom enough times in life to know that I need to follow Johnny and his Aloha Spirit to the North Shore. Yet, I have also learned enough from my stranded state of desperate stable social retardation to say no. There are few places in this world where a magical moment occurs and another human lets you into their culture and lifestyle without even knowing your name, yet we all say no. For all he knows, I am some broken-hearted deadbeat who broke up with his girlfriend in Europe and has been wandering the waterways of Venice, drowning every step of the way. For all he knows, all that I know, I am some poser who once surfed and then abandoned all that was good in life some years ago when I traded my Toyota Tacoma for a Lexus and a six-speed stick shift up my ass because five couldn't quite create enough options for the amount of asshole I had. I have photos of my old self, but I have misplaced them or traded them with others through online conversations and dates. I have lost my identity and all I know is that I am lost and lost is me. Johnny doesn't care.

He has a kind face, and his skin shines with a brilliant bronze glow that seems to liberate the frowns surrounding him. There is an infectious likeableness to him—even before he opened his mouth to utter another line of pigeon Hawai'ian, one could tell that the truth to his happiness was more ambiguous than the Mona Lisa's smile lines. Johnny is the kind of person who holds many keys to many doors, some of which he has walked through, and some of which he has not—not for reasons of insecurity, but for reasons of respect. His hair is a tangled blond mess like seaweed on the ocean floor gripping onto some form of reef that gives way to a bountiful fountain of youth in the depths of land below. His body resembles that of the earth: strong, muscular, scorched, and lined with intricacies that one can only notice from thirty thousand feet above sea level. He fools the mind's eye, making you think you are looking at an element of the earth when in reality what is inside is every ion of the ocean.

I feel safe thirty thousand feet above the earth. Often my body, becoming restless, prays for turbulence so that it can awaken from the feeling that it is in a stable, grounded environment. It's the impermanency I see when I look out the window of an airplane that gives rise to this feeling. Clouds come, clouds pass, as do the land and the ocean below, with no real hesitation. Travelling at speeds greater than the common man knew some one hundred years ago, I can see why people become pilots. A guide and Bodhi in the sky, pilots often share the same characteristics of devout Buddhists, leaving their attachments behind as they take long trips across the world and sharing, most of the time unintentionally, a piece of the truth that is impermanence. Up above the world, we fly with the presence of giants yet think with the mind of a lamb: soft, gentle, empty.

I look across the aisle at my new proposition. His head is hanging heavily, and I wonder for a moment if he is fleeing some mental execution on the mainland like I am. This leads to fact number three regarding airplanes: if one were to commit their mind to the multitude of emotions below an aircraft, they would certainly end up with a steel pipe between their lips and a note that reads, *I have it too good, it just isn't fair for me to live this way knowing what I know now.*

There is a lot of suffering in this world, and it is not just limited to the human species. The ocean is teeming with suffering as our ever-increasing plastic landmass slowly devours the salt landscape that is the home to many a sentient being. When humans decided to project their anthropocentrism upon this world, they made themselves less enlightened than stone. I find myself peering across the aisle at an old man, calm and collected with not a twitch or urge in his settled bones to move. I can't clearly see his face, but I think that he knows, or at least I pretend that he knows, at minimum one answer to the enigma that is living. Possibly and hopefully, he has ascertained some seed of knowledge in his long years that allows him to sit so peacefully over such suffering below. Is his mind racing? Or is he calmer than the moment after a wave breaks? With this thought, Johnny's voice, describing some wave I would surely miss if I end up on Big Island, dissipates into the hurricane of engine hums that guide me into my favourite form of sleep.

CHAPTER ??

With a flash as brilliant as a solar flare, I awake from a bizarre scene of six people situated in a circle, speaking of regrets, short-term goals, and what they wished to accomplish before they passed. The windows of my dream were large, much larger than the ones on this airplane, and they had the same trim as the ones at the airport: brilliant silver, reflecting the little positive energy that was in the room—a silver lining, if you will. The faces were fuzzy but familiar; perhaps these are reflections of people from my past, wishing me well on my way. I sure hope they understand. Just as quickly as I had fallen into my solar revelation, Johnny's voice becomes fact and breaks the droning silence of the jet engines once again.

"Brahdah, man, we getting close to the island, moana is speaking to us, Pele and Kamehameha must approve of you. Check it, we got perfect swell rolling in from the north-northwest and the offshores are picking up, it's a blessing, brah." Johnny is hiding his dated and sun-worn cellphone as he listens to the swell forecast for the coming week. We must be getting close if he has reception.

Having abandoned all certainty that I would be going to Big Island, I ask if Pipeline will be firing, somewhat scared of his answer because if it would be, I may be paddling out into my deathbed.

"Shoots, yeah, if we lucky, brah, we go."

A flight attendant suddenly grasps Johnny's arm and demands that he hang up his phone immediately. She doesn't have the angelic tone of the Spanish woman on the intercom that I'm used to, but she does have enough sexuality in her to make me sweat at the realization that after ten years, I will now have to try to get laid.

I'm not sure what makes a man sweat more — the idea of dropping into one of the world's most deadly waves with caverns six feet below the ocean's surface containing unforgiving teeth built to cut even the most senior of Da Hui, or asking a girl on a date after ten years of monogamous female familiarity. Either way, I have a feeling that this internal enigma is going to bleed out sooner than I can mentally cope with. Sometimes the physicality of being a human outweighs the psychological warnings and we get swept up into a lust-filled dream of bending a flight attendant over the cockpit of a plane, hoping that thirty thousand feet works as a functional contraceptive.

Much like the ocean, women have the power of a certain tranquility that can demand the male soul to shift in patterns across mediums so drastic as to make him feel like he is divine one second and in need of therapy the next. Like the ocean, women demand a certain degree of focus and attention when a man submerges himself in them; for if he takes his eyes away from her, he not only turns his back on a

107

soul-saving possibility, he opens himself to a suffering that is incomprehensible to most who refuse to experience either of these worldly creations. The seven wonders of the world are mere replicas of the power these two beings hold: the power of creation and the power of destruction. My mind is hell-bent on the thought of finding a fast female partner when the Islands break into my mind through Johnny's smile — a smile that says, *Relax, let it come.*

Johnny puts his phone down with a meticulously sculpted smile that took years of living on the Islands to attain. "This is your lucky day," he says with a chuckle as the flight attendant walks away, taking a turn-around glance at my pale white face, which contrasted hers and Johnny's like snow on lava rock.

"Ha. Yeah, I guess, hey. Pretty good-looking." I can hear the uncertainty in my voice, an uncertainty that has been left there by my foolish decision to turn my back on the girl I love, a decision that I had learned how to make initially when I turned my back on the ocean ten years ago. She is destroying me year by year, letting me know that I have just missed another wave that I will regret until she offers up another one. I hope that the woman I left isn't of the same nature.

"Hey, no worries, brah. Aloha, we here."

CHAPTER ?

Honolulu International is one of the most peaceful airports for half of the year, with young surf travellers searching for a taste of the green room and older poets hoping to suck words out of the island's used crust and air. The other half of the year is complete madness, with children running around with fake leis draped around their necks and tired parents yelling at them to collect the baggage containing items that hopefully do the proper job of making nonresidents feel right at home. I look across the terminal and spot my surfboard resting up against the wall next to six others, five of which look like they have already seen the inside of a lava tube. I open its protective bag only to find that my board had been smashed, the rails resembling broken windows and the foam looking as if a dog had been gnawing on it the entire flight. Through my rising anger comes Johnny's voice to my left.

"Shoots, brah, I'm sorry, they got you good, yeah."

I don't know how to respond, my anger is tainting the view of this world already.

"Yeah, fuck'n fuck-ass shit, fuck'n cunts, man!"

"Well, brah," Johnny chuckles, "certainly see you got a good education back home, ya? All good, brah, that board is no good for North Shore anyways — too wide and glass looks too thin, we get you set up, always a bright side, ha, I swear, brah, that board was gonna end up that way whether the airlines mashed it or the reef, too big, yep, too wide for sure."

His words lighten the air in my lungs and allow the blues, greens, and yellows to pierce the cones in my eyes, providing a taste of the insight this man has when it comes to dealing with suffering. He's seen a lot, I think, and I exit the terminal and step into the warm light.

Johnny abandons his role as tour guide to my left, and as I lose sight of him I feel a small, piercing pain of anxiety run through me when I think about what I'm doing here instead of taking the next island hopper over to Hilo. My hand automatically shoots out into the warm air, guiding over a taxi with a distinguished mainland, New York–style gesture. I try to remember the name of the campground Johnny recommended, but my mind falters. I begin to lose sight of colours as they once again drain from my eyes. I place my unsalvageable board through the trunk and over the folded-down back seat, throwing my bag with haste into the remaining space beside my disappointment. As I begin to pull myself into the cab next to it all and attempt to coax the name of where I am headed back into my head, a large truck rolls up in front of the cab, surfboards hanging from the tailgate like children on a farm. It's Johnny.

"Chee, brah! Get outta that cab, we go rippin' up da coast, many dollars up to Malaekahana from here, brah! Haha, shoots you comin' with me, you comin' with me. Thanks, boss, this haole is wit me, you pao, I got dis one."

The cab driver, listening to "Beach in Hawai'i" by Ziggy Marley, knows every word that permeates my ignorant eardrums, and I find myself shifting into the colourful description of the Hawai'ian islands that every tour guide provides with a 100 percent guarantee.

"Uh, sorry, man. Yeah, I guess I go with him, sorry. Uh, shit. Sorry."

"No drama, brah, enjoy your stay. Aloha!"

The drive up the coast is greens, it is yellows, it is plumerias, it is palm trees, it is love at first sight and the promise of a better minute, one after the next. Fuck psychoanalysis, a man can sit with a therapist for hours, days, years, but all he really needs is a piece of this, a sheer moment of distraction from the department store elevator songs and the stale crispness of long-expired bread. I drown my gaze in the sights of reef-torn shoreline and waves breaking one set after the next in perfect unison all along the highway. I fight the urge to ask Johnny to pull over and let me jump in and paddle out into the middle of nowhere and lose myself like the Eddie Aikaus of late before remembering that my board is a shambled mess of foam and glass. He looks over at me and tells me that my face is losing lines and growing young in the shadow of the island's formidable capacity to over inspire.

***

I don't know what I was expecting. I look around at the property, eyes wide open to the possibilities that exist on such a small parcel of land. The dirt road that led up to Johnny's house was rougher than a bus ride in Cambodia. All along the side of the driveway where the lush green vegetation met the dark earth, there were signs and stickers naming in which direction and how far away the most famous surf breaks in the world are. Through the dust in my nose, sun in my eyes, and uncertainty in my mind, I was able to take, for the first time in months, a breath of the possibilities that I now had as I drove further into the blue, green, and yellow unknown.

His house is honest, situated on a small hill that rolls its way down through a garden appearing to contain everything needed to maintain a lifestyle built on salty skin and a protein diet. At the left side of the garden, extending its fingers down into the dark earth, is a banyan tree with a rope hammock meticulously placed between two of its larger arms, which seem to reach out in a gesture of welcoming and comfort. I have never seen such a tree in my entire life, and I have never experienced a plant with such jovial existence. Past the banyan, the garden gives way to thick rainforest, which draws on my mind like a whisper, taunting me to enter and submerge myself in its dreams and allow it into mine.

The property is every mainland surfer's archetypal dream. No two-hour drives in the freezing rain to find boulder-ridden beaches with short, rarely punchy reefs. Here, only the whitest of sand gives way to colourful reef, which bends the swell into perfectly gutted pits, folding over themselves, spitting with such force as to make the Kona winds jealous.

Johnny's place is up through the hills close to a wave known as Velzyland, which was only a five-minute drive down to the world-famous Banzai Pipeline as well as Backdoor, Off-the-Wall, and Gas Chambers, to name a few. The place was littered with waves like the mainland was littered with monetarily righteous people. Standing in the open air with the warm island dirt stuck to my now-reddening skin, it immediately occurs to me that no matter what Hollywood and tourism have tried to do to this place, it is still magical.

"So, what do you think, brah?"

"Johnny, mate, this place is unreal. I, I can't really…yeah."

"Haha, cherry, brah, you can camp over there next to the banyan, sleep in da trees and make friends, brah, it's the island way. You must get to know Pele, and then we will talk to *moana*." I assume he is referring to the land and ocean, as in my brief passings with other surfers I had gathered that moana was something special to Polynesian watermen.

"Cherry, brah," I find myself saying — and immediately regretting.

Johnny must have seen my uncomfortable realization because he laughed and said, "Yeah, brah, reeeal cherry."

The original plan had been to lock up a campsite around the peninsula on the North Shore, about twenty minutes away from where Johnny lives. Yet within that first hour of driving up the

Kamehameha highway, Johnny explained that I had a good mixture of blood and ocean in my veins and that I could stay with him. Hawai'ians have a way of understanding that is far beyond what most of us even try to consider a capable way of being. They have a way of looking at the world through dark brown eyes that not only see what is around them but also feel it, touch it, smell it, and know it. It's an awareness that, prior to the Western invasion, truly believed in innocence until proven guilty. This can still be found in the Hawai'ian culture — albeit a lot less when you're fighting for waves as a haole. But it can still be found. It's a culture shaped in defence to the trespasses against it; but in some beautiful way, it manages to keep its blood true, living like the banyan, offering its arms out to those who care to open their hearts. With extreme uncertainty comes the chance to begin all over again, and I have accidently stumbled into a culture which is conducive to something that I have long been searching for.

I smile.

CHAPTER ???

O'ahu literally means "The Gathering Place," and within the first month of it occupying my mind, body, and soul, I could see why. The weekend market outside of Haleiwa was bustling with tourists coming and going, buying cool sips of kava, and laughing at how relaxed they were as the drink slowly removed them from the anxious city mindset they were used to. Everywhere you could find the Aloha here, not just in the finely crafted items for sale that boasted the colours of the Hawai'ian Islands but also in the smiles and tears of the children tugging on earth-made blankets — ones that cannot be matched in their ability to keep the soul warm. Here, people laugh and cry for the right reasons, it is not always for the misfortunes they have created for themselves (which, like anywhere in the physical world, still do exist), but more often than not tears are shed here in remembrance and in realization that things, like the face of a wave, will inevitably end.

I met Kai by accident on a Sunday in the market after a surf at Ehukai Beach. He is a tall man with the features of a Polynesian chief, the kind that beam over you and make you immediately accept

115

that he is of greatness and deserves to be held in your highest regard—except he would laugh at you and make you a bowl of kava if you ever told him you felt this way. His dark eyes have lightness in them that forms a comforting aura within his demeanour when he speaks. He is a man of compassion and patience on land, but in the water he is a hell-hound who takes double overhead Pipe on the head just to sneak a few seconds of shack time inside what could be a total closeout.

We met out of chance; I was helping a young grom find his dad, a man he described as a warrior, and when we found him, I could see why. Kai approached us with a big island smile lacking any of the anxious expression you would expect to find on a man who had supposedly lost his child. In an attempt to ease the anxiety that obviously wasn't there, I greeted the man.

"Uh, hey, is this your son?"

"Hey, brah! Howz it? Any good waves?" He points at my board, which is nose down in the sand, fins in the air.

"Yeah, brah, real good, actually. Took a few on the head, but you know, moana takes and she gives." I hear Johnny's words coming out of my mouth.

"Shoots! You at Pipe today? It's firing, yeah?"

"Ah nah, brah, I been waiting on that one. You know, gotta have respect for that reef or it'll kill you. I've been surfing just down the beach at Pupukea." I am striving to gain this man's respect as a waterman from the mainland with newly developed island skin.

116

"Haha, like every mainlander, yeah? Build it up and never go out, come on, we go, Pipe is busy, but I've got some time to show you some real hollow stuff later tonight at sundown, what do you say to a red-light session at five o'clock?"

"Is that island time?" I joke, hoping he won't take offence.

He lets out a huge, deep chuckle, one that resembles the thump waves make as they crash down over first reef Pipe.

"Four o'clock island time, brah."

Just then, Johnny runs up with the usual stoke emanating from every pore on his body. "Making friends without me, hey, brahdah man? Haha, howz it, Kai, score any shack time today? Backdoor looks good, I know you like those rights."

I'm a bit taken back that Johnny knows my latest five-minute friend, yet at the same time I'm not surprised at all; O'ahu — The Gathering Place — the idea continues to pursue my thoughts.

"Johnny, how's your family, still charging in those American tours?" Kai asks with a slight hint of distaste on his tongue.

"No, not so much anymore, my brother lives in Australia now as a barrister and my dad has moved back to the mainland again…New York."

"Ah, so the island has left his body again. Sad to hear, he was a good waterman with lots of salt in his blood. That guy could forecast an incoming swell two days before any of this new technology knew there was a low-pressure system brewing. I guess a man has a breaking point, though, can't blame him after…"

117

At this moment I realize I haven't even asked or wondered where Johnny's family is or who they are. I feel foolish, unappreciative, and above all else disrespectful and undeserving of his hospitality.

Johnny gives Kai a nod and changes the subject. "I hear Spot X might go tomorrow…we go and show this haole some real waves."

Kai nods with a grin, looks at me, and says, "Tonight's red-light session will have to wait, you'll need your rest for tomorrow morning."

In this, I realize that I am Johnny's friend *because* I didn't ask about his family, that everything between us is good because I am the impartial jury to his life — the man without any intention to raise unspoken demons and the boy who just wants to learn and play in the ocean. These attributes are the exact reasons I am about to get myself in over my head come first light.

Kai doesn't grab or guide his son by the wrist let alone strap a wristband on his arm and lead him back to his lifted Toyota Tacoma, which boasts tires taller than two of his sons standing atop one another. He nods and his son gives him a look of youth and disobedience, which is aptly met with a smile from Kai and an obvious recognition that his son's defiance is a natural part of his upbringing. Kai rejoices in the opposition before picking his son up, wrestling him playfully, and throwing him into the flat bed of his truck next to his dog, which almost matches the black truck in size.

"Always fuckin' around, yeah? Haha, grom's gonna be a charger someday." Johnny clearly appreciates the pure way in which Kai relates with his son. I wonder if his father is like Kai, or if Kai is the father Johnny has always wanted. I begin to feel that maybe if mine had acted a bit more my age when I was eleven, I would still visit him.

CHAPTER ????

Early morning surf sessions, or blue-light sessions, are often the most nerve-wracking but are also often the most rewarding. As I lie in my banyan hammock, I turn the backlight of my tidal watch on to see how many hours of rest I have before certain death: 3:45 a.m. Fuck, I can't sleep, and that's exactly what I need to be doing.

The Kona winds are heavy, blowing straight offshore towards the spot we are supposed to be surfing in the morning. The moon is a mirror, directing light upon everything resting peacefully below, except for the man rustling around in his hammock on a small island in the middle of the Pacific. As much as I love surfing, Kai—with his grin, his stoke, and his ideas of surfing large waves—have me wishing I am an astronaut drifting far above the earth, looking down on the things that can kill me and frothing in the fact that they can't touch me a million miles above them. But this is here, and this is now, and I have to grow—as much as I don't want to.

The hours remain relentless; I lie here at their mercy as the starlight continues to withhold the relief

120

it has offered to stranded mariners and people of the sea for centuries. Why me, why can't it ease my soul right now? The answer is in the reality of the situation: I cannot receive the relief it offers because relief before you paddle out and surf a bomby is a killer.

It's all part of the preparation, I justify, as the moon tips its hat behind the horizon and the sun begins to drench the earth with life, seeping into every leaf, blade of grass, and strand of hair on every sentient being that I am slowly learning to acknowledge.

As I rise from my hammock, my feet press nervously into the ridged soil, feeling every sharp rock and stick stuck to the earth. My feet have begun to callus from all the reef walking I've been doing in the last few weeks, but for some reason, this morning I can feel everything, and it transfers from my feet through my body and into my nervous, shaky existence.

"Shoots, brah, you don't look so good." I hear Johnny's energetic voice breach the stillness of the air and puncture the stiffened lobes and hammers of my ears. "Feelin' ripe, or what?"

"Yeah, just a rough sleep. Bit cold, you know?"

"Haha, oh yeah, brah, first time surfing some size in a while always has me uneasy at heart, but don't worry, moana will bring you warmth once you're inside her."

The freckle above Johnny's eyebrow — the one that largely contributed to his ability to get you excited — rose as he held his hands in the air and took in a deep breath. I could tell he thrived off danger, and I wasn't quite sure yet if that was coded into my DNA; the fact that he could relax and laugh at a time like this caused an almost anger in me, and I had never been more jealous of someone else's state of mind in my life. This would continue throughout the course of mine and Johnny's relationship until the day he passed. I, continually frustrated that I couldn't achieve this sense of Aloha, struggled with being caught up in storms, while Johnny found a way to find calm in even the biggest of squalls.

There would be no breakfast until we came back from whatever war we were off to fight today; it was a rule I'd made years ago back home when my crew would stop at the local fast-food jam on the way out to the beach only to lose it all on the mile paddle out to the reef. To this day, I don't understand that blatant sort of wasted money, though I did appreciate my old Lexus. My stomach has become accustomed to this lack of energy — what they say is true in me as well as anyone: when you're in an *Oh shit!* situation, the last thing your body cares about is kicking off a course of digestion. And there were a lot of *Oh shit!* situations on the horizon.

Our vessel is a jet ski with a rescue bed trailing behind like some sort of angel that is being forced into hell, forced into a situation where certain death is the hot ticket on the menu and is offered up with sharp ocean floor to start, a floor resembling serrated knives less forgiving than a bed of nails. I look up from the shallow ocean and feel — for the first time in twenty-four hours — excitement and — for the first time in twenty-four years — peace.

With the ocean breathing foam into my face, we skip over the underlying reef like a flat rock over a calm river. The faces of the ocean floor pass below us, each one offering something more enigmatic than the dark-brown eyes of a woman passing on the street—smiling, yet withholding the fact that she could ruin your world in a blink of the brown. I yell up to Johnny, who is driving the ski, but he can't hear me over the howling Kona winds and the voice of the ocean as we break over its body. After I open my mouth, I am slightly thankful for the fact that he has not been able to hear me as I realize that what I was asking is probably something that would deserve a good laugh and possibly a beating from a North Shore local.

The ski comes to a halt and I peer back at the rescue sled, anxious as I am at the sight in front of us.

Johnny breaks our silence. "Gotta wait for the bigger sets to roll through, reef sucks dry and then floods in cycles between sets, gotta wait for re-flood."

I know what he's talking about. Fuck, I can see what he's talking about. A menacing stretch of dry reef is in front of us, along with a wave on the outside of the break you could fit a Volkswagen inside of. There is a right and a left, breaking perfectly, angelically, over the reef. As we sit here, waiting for a break between sets, I see what is inside my soul, what makes me want to break down and what makes me want to die trying to become a part of. Surfing is truly the melding of one's soul with something tangible on earth. Surfers often joke about how they would prefer getting barrelled over to having sex with super models, and in this case specifically, Johnny can see on my face that my soul is calm even though my face is reading distress. He and I both know, as does the ocean, that Abbey Lee Kershaw can wait.

The reef floods and Johnny hits the throttle between two large pillars of coral and rock. I had been hoping that the entire reef would become submerged below six feet of water, yet all the comfort on offer is just enough for a ski to sneak by without scraping the bottom. As we pull around out back behind the shoulder of the peak, the ocean sits still for us, communicating, at least for a second, that we are now a part of something larger than the daily comings and goings on the hard land we left behind us forty-five minutes ago. I can't help but think that surfing really is the ultimate spiritual guide, that those who can calm their minds in moments like this reap the rewards of a universal energy, one that understands love, selfishness, selflessness, compassion, understanding, hate, and enlightenment. I'm far from as wise as the tongue of a prophet, but I'm as wise as the wisest when it comes to those who understand the comings and goings of the language spoken by the ocean. I am a surfer, and I am about to plunge headfirst into a room—a space in time—that no one but a surfer would care to visit. My body is a bodhisattva, returning over and over to the moments inside a wave that can cause absolute love or total suffering. My body acts for my mind, in memory of my mind, and in selflessness for my mind, and my mind grows like a tree with roots embedded in soils rich with empathy. Like the banyan. My body knows I need this to break free of the frozen confounds of my past. My mind is ready for spring.

"Ayden, are you there?"

124

CHAPTER ?

Spring comes in the form of a roaring army of titans heaving themselves over me as I duck-dive, looking up into the glassy light and resurfacing with salt in my eyes and the grin of love across my face. I align myself with the peak of the reef so I am not caught inside the wave or miss it altogether by sitting too far out back. There is no one out here but Johnny and me and our lifeline, which is bobbing out back behind the reef, our last-minute indicator of how big the next set is going to be.

I had been dreaming and picturing it in my mind for over a day now, imagining the waiting of a few sets before I take off into certain death or certain nirvana. It hits me suddenly when my mind decides for my body that the second wave of the set is one worth risking my life for. The feeling is familiar yet far more powerful than other moments I have had within the ocean. The usual kick of the swell behind me opens the gates to my journey as the offshore winds blows salt into my eyes — a voice of caution and the final gatekeeper to the act I am about to perform in front of the gods.

The lip of the wave snaps hard and fast as the weight of it overpowers its structural stability. I stand up as so many have done long before me in moments of revelation on the great battlefields. My board, with a swift motion, begins to slide down the vertical face of the wave as I see it open up and peel left down a perfect, glistening, heavenly line. My lungs fill with air and I hold it in tightly, like the stratosphere holds in the air for the earth. My eyes fix on the beauty that is before me, and a tear falls. Is it the ocean's tear or my own? As the ocean's face swells beneath my feet, I punch my left hand into its body, grabbing hold of everything I have loved, lost, and come to be, and I hold onto it as the crest of the wave breaks over my head with a sound so loud that it is dead silence to the ears of the child inside me. I look back at my hand as it drags inside the ocean's body, fishing like an ancient mariner for the light of the moon over the water.

I am completely and utterly found.

I let go of the moments I have been so scared to release from inside, and at once the room I am standing in is green, and then silver. People standing around me, whispering thoughts of freedom from a life of suffering, accompany the bright light that pours through the windows to my heart. I am standing in the middle of a great meeting of the mind and body, people looking at me with soft, empathetic smiles gesturing me towards the bright windows. I begin to walk towards the glistening glass fixtures, gripping the soft silk robe I am wearing as it drifts in the ocean breeze. The world is a room filled with a certain reassurance that everything will go on. Some of the faces I have seen before and others I am just getting used to when the light coming through the glass around me surges with angelic tones, and I charge out of the ocean's arms and into a massive cut back, throwing a moment of spray into the world above me and into the next sixty-five years of my life.

Johnny and I surf Spot X until our arms become jelly and our bodies refuse to play into the plan our minds have for it. I take a few giants on the head and a few into memory as Johnny and I look at each other for the first time from the same emotional ground. We call the session. The drive back on the ski seems calmer, tamer, and less unnatural to my body as we skip over the surface that has given me a look through a window into my past, present, and future. I am thankful for all the things around me: Johnny, the ocean, the fish, the air, and, most importantly, my past for driving me into the ocean and out of my concrete box back "home."

Kai is waiting at the dock as we roll up with our four boards and our grins, which portray every moment we have just experienced, leaving nothing out.

"Brah! Certain I missed some bombys, howz it? You get this haole into some size"? He appears excited for us, as if he is feeding off the energy we have brought back from battle.

"This boy can shred!" Johnny says with a tone of surprise that makes you feel the excitement he can't contain. "He even dropped in before I did, claimed it!"

"True island style, good to hear you've finally found your match!" A tingle rises up my spine as he speaks these words. However trivial they may have been to Kai and Johnny, this is my christening as a surfer; respect from an elder waterman is like having a conversation with the creator on these islands.

Kai's truck is parked next to Johnny's, and we load up the ski and boards and discuss the perfect idea of grabbing a quick fix of kava to cool off before carrying on with our day. Johnny's truck grumbles as we haul the ski from the water and drive off down the road. I look back through the rear-view mirror, bare and reef-cut feet dancing out the window as the warm day's air guides my legs up and down. I am still pumping lines in the ocean as the truck makes its way back towards civilization, and I glance one last time towards the break that changed my life.

CHAPTER ?????

The Haleiwa markets are bustling with tourists — a title I am slowly being allowed to relinquish. Through the island's eyes, tourists are mechanisms of economic homeostasis, offering the local population a market to provide primary, secondary, and tertiary services to. They consume hand-squeezed juices and hand-strained kava and embark on flights from Honolulu to Molokai, acting as the central nervous system in the living organism that is the Hawai'ian Islands chain. This central nervous system, including its feedback loops and cellular production sites, is located in the brain that is O'ahu. A tourist's playground, this island offers itself as the gateway to all things that create capital gains in the middle of the Pacific. It is also the home to some of the world's best surfing, offering dark chasms of reef that help mitigate the international crowds that fill up the waters come winter time.

Not far in distance, but marooned in its function and reasoning, is the island of Kaua'i, boasting cliffs on the Napali Coast that fool the spiritual wanderer into thinking that a leap of faith is required in order to obtain release from the grasps of the grey area between heaven and hell. Known as the garden island, Kaua'i is the heartbeat of the island chain and one of the few places in this world where green is the antithesis of envy. Its deep valleys flow with royal eloquence, greeting the ocean with rocky, abrupt, and sharp dissuasive gestures, turning boats away from its shores and inner beauty with a snap image of its form from miles away. In this, Kaua'i remains the locals' terra firma, guarded by the Polynesians of old with rich heritage surrounded by the oldest of ages. Beating the blood of Polynesian ritual and tradition through to the commercialized and capitalized sectors of the Hawai'ian body, Kaua'i is one of the few places that mitigates the Western eye of influence, acting as a lens that colours the heart of the Pacific. Robust with shades of blue and green, it exists in reference to the gardens spoken of in all religious scripture. It is a place of wonder and enchantment, and it is the birthplace of a man I have come to see not only as a friend but as a brother.

Johnny floats over to me through the market crowds, standing out like a flower through weathered cracks of concrete in New York City. His fluidity speaks contrary to the expression on his face, which speaks of distress. His pupils are dilated and his skin is pulsing out beads of sweat that form over his brow like a crown of anxiety. Through the horde of people pushing and pulling between the energies of O'ahu and Kaua'i, Johnny collapses. Like a defeated king, he comes crashing down with a defiance of gravity that is earth shattering.

I grab hold of his singlet, tearing it slightly around his armpit as I pull him to his feet. He is wasted, I realize, and it is only 10:30 a.m.

"What the fuck are ya doing, mate?!" I cry out so loud that you would think I am a devout Mormon.

"Shit ain't right, brah, just fuckin' telephones, man, telephones and distances, man, they get me fuckin' down, why can we talk over distances, you know? It's like, fuck, I don't need to hear from a thousand miles away, telephone calls are ruining man, straight up ruining lives every day."

I have no idea what Johnny is talking about, but I grab hold of his arm in a brotherly fashion, wash some kava down his throat with some freshly drained coconut water, and pull him through the mob of humans who all stare at these two scruffy-looking young locals and wonder what the hell has gone wrong in such a beautiful place. I can feel their thoughts as we ignite the flames of reality inside them as we pass. Eyes that speak anger and hearts that would pay handsomely to avoid us guide us out into the busy street. Rental cars pass us as quickly as an affluent tourist would travel through the slums of Mumbai. Bare-footed, I stumble with drunk Johnny over my shoulder across the busy street into a small guarded green area.

Johnny's eyes are yellow with alcohol and his breath is as warm as the inside of a Tahitian barrel; I can feel it on my neck as I lay him down against a large, strong banyan.

"What the fuck happened, Johnny?" I say in a slight bout of compassion mixed with urgency and anger.

"This place is hell, man, that's what he, uh, said, yeah, brah, that's why they left, that's why he called. Fuck 'em!" I am beginning to piece something together in my mind, and it involves his family that he has never mentioned, his past he has never mentioned, his life he has forgotten. The past has a way of breathing its darkness into new light and a way of tainting smiles with haphazard paint strokes of noxious images. If Johnny's current canvas is white, his past canvas is a goddam Jackson Pollock, and the paint is starting to bleed through.

"I just gotta find something, man, I've lost something, you know, brah? When you lose something? Like it was never there, you know? Fuck 'em, brah." He reaches for a branch, misses it, and tumbles over to the ground like a moon shot from the sky. Dust rises around his face, adding to the golden brown texture of his skin a surreal image of the earth combining with man. The sun is hot and the body of Johnny, drained on booze, leaves our conversation shortly after his mind goes out to sea. I pick up his remains and carry him on my shoulder like a soldier walking through the forests of Bastogne—proud to be a brother, yet remorseful for the mind that is slowly deteriorating from years spent between the crosshairs of a nuclear mind fuck. I pull our boards, which have so recently provided us with pure joy, from the back seat of Johnny's truck and replace them with his appealingly lifeless body. I drive with haste down the highway, the rough bit of road leading up to Johnny's place doing nothing to disturb him from his drunken slumber. And to think, I used to be a gin drinker.

CHAPTER ?

It's dark when Johnny finally comes to, lifting his head off the mustard-coloured sofa, which was dropped half-mindfully in the middle of his living room.

"Shoots, what happened, man?" he asks. "I need some water, brah, bring it, yeah?"

I grab a bottle of water from his rusting fridge, the tainted smells of yesterday's dinner wafting out.

"You were out, man, going on about some shit you lost or something," I say, trying to keep my tone casual and pretending I don't know of the internal war he has just come out of. "Were, were you on the phone with someone? You were talking about someone, you seemed pretty upset, man." I speak in an almost therapeutic tone, as if I had established our relationship within one sentence and was now ready for some cognitive behavioural therapy to begin.

"It's fine, I don't want to breathe fire into that, call it 'daddy issues,' brah, write it off, let's night surf." Johnny gets up in spite of the pain that is seeping through his pores and grabs his quad fish. "We go, brah, we go."

That day I realized that most things in this world die before they become something beautiful. In Johnny's case, I would later learn through a paint-by-numbers map that his dad had been a great wave charger — one of the islands' best. Competing in the WQS for a number of years before meeting Johnny's mum, he'd had the dream Johnny would be chasing if it weren't for his father's living, breathing cocaine addiction, which consistently served as a sour lemon within the drink that was Johnny's ocean.

His mum had died in a car accident five years after Johnny was born, he and his father barely making it out alive. His father bore the truthful existence that he was the root of the pain Johnny lived every day, being high at the time of the crash. They'd been travelling from a corporate-sponsored surfing documentary screening in Ala Moana, a film that boasted some of the best surfers on the island, including Johnny's dad, Manoa himself. The film had taken Manoa's head and driven a spike of platitudes through it and onto his tongue, expressing everything he cared about with great ownership and hostility.

Johnny's mother, Lokelani, with her opulent hair that formed to every square inch of the ocean's breath, was from old money and thus a high-standing citizen within the Honolulu community. She had letters from just about every man who would be willing to turn their hearts away from their wives and bend them to meet hers. Manoa had the eyes Lokelani had desired since they'd met at Sunset Beach when she was visiting on a school fundraising trip for the less well-supported North Shore schools. Manoa had just finished a session and was sitting on the back of his 1954 Land Cruiser with a plantain in his mouth and a fistful of change that was to feed his wave-hungry stomach for the next week.

As any romance worthy of telling goes, Manoa approached Lokelani with his last banana and a smile that could turn the affluent girl from complacence in riches to happiness in rags. His high and dense eyebrows offered a soft touch to the stringy yet hardened body that lunged the man into the deepest caves one could find when hitting the reefs surrounding O'ahu. She had no idea who he was, and he knew only one thing of her: she was moana, the ocean he searched for every day when he paddled out. Sometimes frothy and unforgiving, sometimes smooth to the touch and easy to get inside, she was perfection. It was only a matter of time before Manoa began to make the long trips down to Honolulu to visit, always with a weathered fistful of plumerias picked from gardens surrounding his house. Johnny's house.

Working in the fields between the South and North Shores, Manoa's family was rich in beauty yet poor in the eyes of those who held Western power in the political arena on the southern front of the island. It was a time of political shift and there was a push to Westernize the island for tourism purposes, increasing the overall quality of living for the select few in the urban centre. Manoa cared nothing for politics, for he had within him the courage of Kamehameha and the heart of Pele. But if one were to look back, one would certainly see that Lokelani gave him the latter, for Manoa's past was riddled

ALEXANDER HOLT

with domestic violence and the violence between his friends and the rival surfers who had begun to show up from all parts of the world. He was a brambly man with a dangerous heart, a keg of gunpowder waiting for a firing pin.

There was a gentle progress to Manoa and Lokelani's courtship, never moving with haste and always set back by the disapproval of Lokelani's father and his Western influence on her life. Pushing through the socioeconomic disparity became a daily infatuation and a seed that was the growth of their sycamore. Their differences were a great prize waiting over the Nounou mountain range, yet in tragedy these sleeping giants would eventually overtake Manoa by the jealousy forged forever in his heart, a jealousy that would turn him into a power-enthralled man of great searing flame. The fire of injustice may simmer within a man, but it never fails to break free and burn everything around him, for there is no escaping the trespasses upon one's existential pathway to the gates of whatever heaven one should choose. When rocks are moved, they are shattered and the journey becomes a lifelong quest for the steps one has lost.

December 26 was the date Manoa got into a car with a fury inside that not even the greatest of gods could contain. He yelled the entire way back to the North Shore that night, taking the route up along Kaena Point towards Haleiwa with a speed that burnt the air he passed through. Johnny was in the back seat, only five at the time, when the car flew off the road and into the scabrous rock lining the bay. It was low tide and the sea was passively watching as gods covered their eyes in the starry night sky. With a twist of metal and a slam of fate, the car keeled over itself, thrusting the great goddess of Manoa's world face first through the window and into a cavern of rock, where she remains as part of the island to this day. I know this because Johnny's photo album tells of this.

We often visited the cave that held her spirit in the arms of Pele, plumerias of our own in hand — a task passed down to Johnny after his father had left the island for New York to study business administration and that soon became the hatred that would lead to the loss of his own possibility for salvation. Beside the cave, there were always flowers and, most importantly, there laid the last words spoken by Manoa to his wife, which I now know by memory and hold within the caves of my heart next to my own reasons for leaving the grey behind and seeking out my own salvation. The words are those that cannot be replaced by anything mythical or magical, words that are not made of letters but of blood, flesh, tears, and this thing we humans like to call the spirit of humanity. No words ever made more sense to me, and no words would ever come closer throughout my life to bridging the gap between the love of a human and the love of moana.

> *Here lies an island forever in the arms of Pele*
> *And so it was and will be*
> *A line drawn and always removed from the land*
> *That is the territory of your body*
> *And so it was and will be*
> *I lose myself to islands we all wish were long*
> *forgotten*

I had become involved in and one with Johnny's past, present, and future; I had become one with something more powerful than any man sitting in a hospice would ever be able to feel while staring up at metallic birds as they passed by the silver-lined windows. I had experienced it, as I had the photos in my mind to prove it.

CHAPTER ???

Lying in this bed with white curtains hanging off brass rods like the drapes of the Lusitania, the light shines brightly as it always does when I fall into lucidity and into the actual reality of my life. I am old — my skin shows it and my mind acts it as I try to force out some stormy memory of my own. Is it the boat I sailed across the world in or the barrels I explored with the smile of the five-year-old I never was? A confused old man lying with a catheter for a lover and an intravenous as a friend by his bed is not how I ever expected to see myself. I don't think the world will ever realize that wrinkles haven't always been the terrain of the expired. We were once men, great explorers of men, with girls we liked to fuck and dreams we chased and shattered and learned to love by. Well, I think maybe this was my life — at this point nothing really makes much sense anymore, and who I am and will be for my remaining days is to be determined by the decomposition of my sanity and the memories of my subjective reality in a space and time where I am lost. A lone star sucked into the

139

darkness of space, where nothing ever comes back.
Especially prayers.

CHAPTER ??

I have learned a lot from the islands of
Hawai'i; I have learned of the channels of current
that separate the tourists from the locals and of the
dollar signs that separate the enlightened from the
protected. Above all else, I have learned of the heart
and what it means to have a place to belong.
Johnny's past is my past, and my past slowly
becomes his as we explore, like psychoanalysts high
on salt water, the depths of each other's oceans.

It's a Friday and I have just finished work at
the juice bar I had taken a liking to when I first
arrived on the island. Squeezing kava root and
making juice bowls is now my way of making
amends with capitalism, getting by rather than
getting ahead and sucked back into the life I ran
away from. The air is filled with fresh sugar straight
from the roots of the island, and the café is bustling
with locals and keen tourists eager to find a piece of
the real Hawai'i. I look out past the juice bar and
count five faces that my mind traces and labels as
familiar, all of who were born within thirty minutes
of the café. Dollars are exchanged for sips of the
earth, and I make my honest wage always knowing

that the real payment for my service behind the bar is in the relationships I am building. It isn't a California sun that breaks through the stained glass windowpanes onto the tables and across the floors; it is a sun that comes from within the locals who have begun to accept me as a son of the islands. I wring out a bag of kava root into a large pail of water, watching the brown, illustrious liquid turn the water into a tranquil ocean of peace before me. I serve each scoop into a coconut shell and rest it upon the beaded bracelets we allow customers to take for a small donation to SurfAid. This is our way of giving back; this is our way of showing the earth a token of our appreciation for the peace it offers us every day.

There are the regular locals I have a mutual fondness for, and then there are the assholes who are on the extreme opposite end of the suit–board short dichotomy. These guys will never accept me, and this is the hardest thing I will have to come to terms with if I ever want to blend in with this world. "These guys don't even accept *me* because my dad is from the mainland, brah," Johnny once told me, assuring me that the stiff upper lips cast in my direction were simply placed there by King Kamehameha to balance out the suits that breed larger and larger every year within the central business district of Honolulu.

I am all fine and well with the acceptance of these things on land, but in the water I am a fierce warrior for equality, which would be taken as disrespectful if it wasn't true that I am slowly being absorbed into the social fabric with each break from Diamond Head to V-Land and beyond. I owe a lot to this little juice bar and my best friend, Johnny. It is true what they say about these islands: it may be

142

localized, but the locals are true at heart if yours aligns with theirs. One man had led me headfirst into a life that not even multimillion-dollar blockbusters can capture accurately. I don't think many places in this world can place that on their resumé.

"Howzit, brah?" Johnny approaches me with a smile brightened by the island's finest weed. "You pau? Gettin'all akamai up in here."

"Fuck, howzit, brah? Juicing is da kine, haha. Fuck, wish I wasn't working, I don' know how you manage to surf all day, be looking moke, brah, getting them muscles in prime shape for Pipe Master trials, hey?"

I have become one with who I had been afraid to be for the first twenty-five years of my life. I have put down the suit, the fine dining, and the expensive flowers imported from places most can only dream of going. Every plumeria I see on the North Shore reminds me of the ones I paid over one hundred dollars to import for my girlfriend, my fiancée, back where I came from.

"Shoots! Haha, yeah, brah," says Johnny. "Getting all moke for real, gotta be as strong as the wave to surf it." It's little statements like these that continually turn my face and heart into a smile. "For real though, I've got some news for you, brah, might not like it, but it's come through the wind to you and you should give it the time of day. 'Spect you won't be too chill about it, but hey, sa'll where we be at, brah." His voice is cryptic and somewhat concerned for what might happen to me within the next few hours. He can tell that my heart is weary and that the threat of anything coming across the wind in my direction other than swell surely places a heavy

143

weight upon my mind. "All good, brah, think you might be happy," he says. "Shoots, real happy, haha!"

I am at home away from it all, but on this day, the past pays me a swift Kona wind and takes me off my feet like a Western Yogi actualizing the reason for the air he is breathing.

"Brah, we go, she's waiting for you back at the place." One foot after the other, I find myself leaving the juice bar, looking back through the wave-painted windows as the sun casts its shadow to dusk against them, and I wonder if I will ever enter that door again as the same man.

***

It hits me harder than sixty-foot Jaws as she walks through the doorway and back into the pathway of my life. I can feel and sense the flow of her as an old sailor feels the one voyage that almost claims his life. The moment is now, the moment that can be provided with no bearing, no longitude, no latitude, and with absolute certainty no words to describe it. My ship sinks deep into the trough of a wave as she approaches me like a stranger in a lucid dream. Her feet glide softly over the mortar floor, treading lightly but with intention, each step coming closer and closer to my heart and its anchor, outstretched, reaching for the bottom of our world together ten thousand leagues below the sea. Like some distant parallel universe colliding deep in space, we embrace without word or explosion but with a bittersweet ignition of desire in the forefront of the existence I have created for myself on these islands. She pulls her body back from me, leaving a trace of her sweet perfume to linger with my senses.

144

Her eyes are posted up to the world like two purple gems held up against a Moroccan skyline. I can feel no other presence in the room other than that offered by all my senses and my recollection of everything that was good inside our journey together and where it had begun and ended.

"I didn't expect to ever see you again." I feel my lips permeate the intensity of the conversation our minds and bodies are caught in. "I mean, I'd hoped you'd decide — Well, I never thought you would decide this, not saying that you'll be here forever or anything, but — " I tremble and stumble into my mainland dialect. "It's good to see you, Marielle."

Sitting on the front porch of Johnny's place, the Hawai'an sun turns its back on me as it drops well below the crest of the waves. My legs are jittering, but not with anxiety or uneasiness — the island has taught me how to fight these feelings. They are jumping up and down along with my thoughts, which are with the final barrels that I can hear crashing against the shallow reef in the distance; they are jittering because for once I have found myself and not someone else within me. I find myself vocalizing this in conversation with Marielle as I explain with heated intensity what I have learned and what I want to do with it. She entertains my words like a child at the circus, smiling and nodding as if my being is a stop on her tour's itinerary. *To our left is the real deal, folks! He's a real surfer, and he even works at a juice bar!* My thoughts betray me, and I begin to consider that maybe my life has involved a few ounces of irresponsibility mixed in with multiple parts of spiritual revelation.

"But, Ayden, this isn't who you are," comes a whisper from the deepest, darkest depths of the oceans bowls.

"And how the fuck would you know?"

CHAPTER ???

I spend a long Hawai'ian day wondering where I am from and where I am going. I consider my *ohana* — my family — here, and I consider the potential family I could have with Marielle. Kids, a dog, and a stable job that would allow me to obtain all the great Western provisions that World War Every Time attempts to protect by breaking the backs and bodies of the world. So many suffer for such comforts that so often don't even come close to touching the truth that is the bond of ohana. Everyone is my uncle and auntie, there are no predefined lines of some blunted nuclear family with a continual bitter taste of regretful responsibility. Ohana is love, and love is a choice. My love for Marielle drove me to faraway lands, but somewhere in between the ideology of Western love and the island's inability to let my heart go, I met with Marielle again on a rainy January afternoon at the café to discuss who I really am and where I would not be going.

"That conversation was a lightning bolt into my heart, your presence here is the piece of thunder that is the palpitation my heart feels. How do I describe this to you?" The café windows are fogging up as the final patrons leave with smiles matching the exact opposite type of cloud that loomed ominously over my stormy words. "Marielle, I can't begin to describe the reason I came here."

"You're a pussy, listen to yourself. This mumbo jumbo Hawai'ian bullshit, you know this state is American soil, right? Ayden? RIGHT?!" Her face is turning away from mine, following the footsteps of the smiles, foreshadow for the final moments of our meaning on this planet.

"You know, you fucking asshole," she continues, "you're just like your father, the man you say was a war hero but who really fled the great nation of America for some lost island in the sun. A bunch of real fucking hippies—I would call you a lost soul in wanderlust, but that would romanticize and outline the precision of your choices too nicely, you're just an idiot who wouldn't know an ever-after kiss if a girl gave you one." She reaches over and pulls my lips into hers, into that warm chasm of lustful, wishful thinking I had been yearning for in every moment up until this one. I have flashbacks as my father would have had if he had made it to war, but she is right, he was a draft dodger and the reason I have come here. I'm dodging my own draft, but the war I'm avoiding is to last in me forever. It isn't 1940-something, and airplane tickets have the potential to bring worse wars for the low cost of an economy ticket on any major airline.

"Why now? Why the fuck now, Marielle? Why not a year ago? Why start the war! Why start the war now, you fucking magnificent, ignorant, fucking fuck!" I'm at a loss for words and the English dictionary is a surgeon's handbook that is too difficult for me to bother with. I have forgotten all at once that I had left Marielle, despite the mutual distaste we had instilled in one another.

"Because I love you, Ayden! Loved.… Now that I see you here, you and your father's ways, this life you have here, it's so…*pathetic* it makes me sick." The wind begins to batter the small café's windows as the final cars pull out from the North Shore parking lot, leaving us alone with the slow music playing over the speakers up in the corner of the room. The silence puts the clatter of mugs and bagel plates on full presentation, which complements the slowly growing melancholy of our storm and the music from above. I hear a truck start up outside, a loud booming noise protruding into our perfect little fuck show. I don't need to look twice to realize it's Johnny's old friend Zack, a guy I am not fond of but know well enough to ask for a ride back to Johnny's.

"Then that's that." The words rush from my lips. "Some final destinations in our hearts teach us that final destinations are nonexistent—happy or sad. Goodbye, Marielle, and don't forget to buy your plastic lei and dancing hula girl at the airport." Rushed words, but worthy of a life's story, or at least a few photos in a photo album.

I push the café door open, allowing the rain to crash into me, beads of the ocean tasting my hot skin, being treated to the true joke of humanity. So much beauty outside yet such a strong ability to turn it all to shit, we humans, the capable ones, always know how to make a storm worse than it really is.

"You got a ride, brah?"

"Fuckin' stranded."

149

CHAPTER ?

Even in paradise the devil himself has a name and a face. His parade always begins with an inky, rich black hue that rips the colour from the bountiful blue skies above, a poignant front soon followed by a storm that buries reefs in sand and sinks the brightest hearts with its malice. This storm ripping through my life is not a literal low-pressure weather system. I wish it were. It isn't even my brief encounter with Marielle, which has left me stranded on an overpopulated island in the Pacific for a few weeks' time, her words still ravaging the neural pathways in my jumbled head. But that photo has been cut and pasted onto a timeline that had come to pass.

Evil presents itself in the form of Johnny's departure from O'ahu, creating a ripple effect that leaves my life spinning out of control. My attempts to find a place to stay — a place that can foster and facilitate the presence of positivity, a place that will allow me to continue to live out what Marielle had promised me was a fake parallel universe — are thwarted by the fact that I am living in an expensive

150

time on minimum wage. The job I declined on Big Island begins to bite at my coattails.

Johnny had left to find work on the mainland and his grandfather took control of the farm he was living on — that we were living on. Johnny had tasted the cold feeling that most residents in Hawai'i taste, unless of course they are from new money. It's a flavour that tastes like the ink from a well-used American one-dollar bill — a gritty, dirty taste that forces even the most peaceful Hawai'ian into frustration and leaving home. This was the same taste his father had feasted on. The taste of debt. Debt and rising property taxes were the two individuals who opened the ninth gate and called upon Hawai'ian Satan to come and begin to devour my peaceful state of mind. Things wouldn't be so bad if the only place I could afford on a juice-bar budget wasn't a cocaine-, Xanax- and alcohol-infused residence owned by a mainlander from Beeville, Texas.

Zack Pettucia: a man with more anger than the heart of a million burning suns and a vocabulary that failed to exceed that of a sexually frustrated and confused ninth-grade child. His budget is subsidized by his father, who is a large tycoon in the oil field in Beeville, a man who has no idea what the word *parent* means outside of providing large sums of money for the pockets of every drug dealer from Waikiki to Kaneohe. Zack Pettucia: a child with no concept of reality, still taking on tenth-grade math at the community college and all the while attempting to call himself a local, peacocking and yelling at every white, Japanese, Hispanic, Chinese, and Korean person he sees. He is a child who owns nothing yet thinks he holds the land title to the entire island chain.

I ran into Zack again shortly after Marielle's departure while sitting on the beach at Log Cabins, hoping, like most surfers, that the onshore north westerlies would flop and turn offshore. The day was growing old and tired of being lit up by the sun, so I had decided to wax up and paddle out despite the wind's face when I heard a voice shoot out like the spray of a barrel against the back of my head.

"Are you fucking high? This is shit."

I turn to see eyes that are vaguely imprinted on the inside caverns of my memory.

"Sorry, do I know you?"

"Yeah, faggot, you met me at that party and I drove you home that night. you faggot. You Johnny's friend, yeah?"

I hesitate before replying, "Uh, yeah, man. He's gone though, you know, and yeah, shoots, thanks again."

"Yeah, yeah, Johnny the man is gone, fucking faggot can't surf anyways, island's better off without that haole." His vocal tone smells of drug abuse and insecurity, yet for some reason I entertain his anger.

"Ha, well he grew up here, I don't know if I would call him haole, brah."

"Fuck you, haha! You going surfing in that shit? Fuck that, man, it's for fucking kooks out there, fucking barneys."

I find myself lured in by his negative incantations if for no other reason than that I currently am at a loss for friends to surf with. I paddle out with this guy's eyes tracing my every snap, lay back, and roundhouse before noticing that he too has decided to paddle out. I paddle over and around the line up to greet him, expecting to be met with a smile and a *howz it*. Instead, nothing, no words, just a blank face and an attitude that tells me I am too foreign to bother pretending that he knows me while in the water. I begin to think this man might be a Hawai'ian who has maybe made some bad choices but is capable of knowing the right people to be considered a true local. I find comfort in his distaste for conversation in the water and adopt what we surfers call a pretty decent "stink eye." By the end of the session I am so focused on not being friendly that I find myself not having any fun at all. I turn and catch a wave in, attempting to summon my inner Buddha and relax.

Back on the beach, my living conditions are evident as I pull my surfboard bag and clothes out from under a palm tree.

Zack looks sceptically at me. "You want a ride, brah? Where you living now?"

Welcome to Satan's paradise.

CHAPTER ??

The house has one bedroom that is isolated from the rest of the house. Its cabinets are typical 1990s-style oak with gold handles that once boasted some resemblance of style but are now tarnished, displaying the aging process that salt air has on fashion. The fridge is filled with day-old takeout, sour milk, and Sailor Jerry spiced rum—a bottle that is all too often emptied and replenished thanks to the crude oil money forwarded direct from Beeville with what Zack's father thinks is love. I sleep on a twin mattress outside on the porch that stretches out into a fenced backyard filled with dog shit from Zack's Doberman, Paco. Paco has had an unparalleled anger instilled in him by the continual punches to his face and kicks to his ribs that Zack so lovingly has learned to provide to those he cares for—and to anyone dumb enough to get involved with him.

At night I lay outside and try to find the same feeling that the Kona winds provided to my well-being not six months prior to moving into this drug-infested, mephitic home. But it never works. Outside at night, my ears are constantly bombarded with hollow echoes reminiscent of some true gang documentary filmed in LA, New York, or Las Vegas. The smell of bong hits and charred cocaine mixes with baking soda and permeates every pore of the drywall, and the sight of incomplete community college worksheets litter the scratched-up table that attempts to serve as a humble piece of home inside the dark abyss that sucks the life and light from the Hawai'ian sun. This is home. This is the dark side of the island's reality that I am prepared to live in to keep the dream alive.

The dream that now has the face of a nightmare.

CHAPTER ???

The only bonus of living with Zack is the fact that he has access to the Marine Corps Base, a base that contains surf breaks inaccessible to those without the correct military documentation. Not even Kelly Slater has surfed that area, and to a surf traveller, finding an uncrowded, under-surfed spot in O'ahu is something to give your left nut for.

"Yo, faggot, hurry up, you're so fucking slow. Let's fucking go, we're going to surf Base."

I feel excited every time I hear this, but the lack of vocabulary outside of insult presses hard on my desire to surf with this human. Like usual, we pile our boards into the back of his raised pickup truck, which serves as a symbol for his weakness and a reminder to those on the Kam highway that Satan was about to plow through traffic and take any life that he so pleased. I can't say much to defend myself as he was constantly intoxicated on something while driving, but the drive to the beach was needed to fulfill my desire to surf, which always outweighed my desire to give in, give up, and go back.

"Fuck this, faggot! Move!" Another bout of anger, another drive to the beach. We race between cars, doing California lane changes and almost killing every tourist while we're at it. He pulls out a small pipe and takes a hit of something that is sure to make the drive that much more sketchy.

"Man, fuck these Japs, I call 'em Yaps, you know? Fucking come bomb this island and then fucking come here with cameras and shit, fuck that shit, go home, fucking haoles."

My face is in the permanent form of stagnant swamp water, not revealing a yes or no, just a casual look out the window to the countryside passing by as our hearse of destruction tears through the beauty that I am choking on in attempt to appreciate.

"Hey, so where's best to paddle in and out here?" I ask, hoping to receive an actual answer and not an insult.

"I dunno, man, like look at this shit, got some reef in my neck, been there for ages, from this spot." I know he is a compulsive liar in need of any crutch to add to the formula that makes up his fake Hawai'ian demeanour, but fear still rises within me.

"So, like, left? Right? Which way is the channel?"

"Stop being such a fucking pussy." His words again force my gaze to the side window and my happiness deep into the tar-like oil sands that paid for this kid to live a dream in hostility and anger.

The truck slams over the speed bumps of the military base as we rip past the uniformed guards at the gate and into what appears to be a boot camp mixed with a university for killing. My heart buckles as the truck rattles up to the beach. I can see not-so-perfect lines peeling in off the sand bars out behind the inner reef that I will soon have to negotiate like a solider making his way through guerrilla warfare in the middle of Vietnam.

"It's cold, this is gay, this surf sucks." More negative chanting fills the cab of the truck and I struggle not to yell at him to shut the fuck up. I am a matador hiding his cape from the bull, but I know that I will eventually have to pull it out if he forces it hard enough.

"All right, man," I say pleasantly and with patience. "I think I'm still going to go out. You can always have some fun even in slop, and you always learn something." My positive energy is immediately met with argument.

"Yeah whatever, man, you're a barney, you'd surf anything."

With no reply, I retire to the rear-end of the truck and rub some sex wax into the glass of my board. With no take on where to paddle out, I observe the currents and jump a rock on the right side of the reef, paddling over ankle-deep reef, determined to show him that I am going to have fun despite his hostility towards the conditions. They really aren't that bad. In fact, with no one else in the water, it soon becomes apparent that Zack doesn't surf that often because in all reality he isn't very good.

I take several lefts and rights after reaching the sandbar out back known as Pyramids and begin to feel a smile come up from the depths to breach my face— those old, familiar lines that once stretched as long as the waves of Raglan and Chicama. My momentary happiness and peace are met with a few military guys who have taken up the sport while serving their time on base. We all have one thing in common, and that is we all know we are lucky to be scoring these waves while everyone and their uncle competes against the crowds on the North Shore. Our session continues into the day as set after set delivers cheers from all those in the lineup. By midafternoon, the swell begins to drop and, sure enough, out paddles Zack.

"Look at these barneys, man, fuckin' longboarder soldier motherfuckers."

They are looking at him and hearing his every word.

"I'm going to drop in on every one of these kooks, go back to Afghanistan," he states with intent to scare.

The session is swallowed up by Zack's coarse, anti-social personality as he ruins everyone's lines by dropping in and taking waves out of position. The looks trace from him to me. Guilty by association, I paddle in — with no run-in with the reef that was surely promised by Zack. His scare tactics begin to show like the stripes on a toothless adolescent tiger. I sit on the beach and watch as more people begin to paddle in, leaving Zack out back by himself, not catching any waves and definitely not appreciating anything. I do have to give the guy some credit, though: he does push off a nice lay back on his last wave before paddling in.

"Brah, I got, like, twenty-five barrels out there," he says as he approaches me. I saw his entire session from the beach and want to spit back in his face that he hadn't even come close to getting covered up.

"I dunno, man, not many barrels out there, I don't know how you found them."

"You gotta know how to surf, man," he snaps back at me, tasting the tip of my disbelief in his skills and his abilities as a true local.

The stares from my fellow comrades in the water, which were once shouts of joy, cast a shadow on my name and face as Zack's truck pulls off into the darkening day. We pass banyans that once made me smile, shrimp trucks that once made my mouth water, and smiles that I now envy. By all standards, I need a change.

We arrive back at Zack's and sit down to watch yet another *Lockdown* documentary on the corruption in correctional facilities in America. Zack Nobody shouts at the television and continues on one uneducated rant after the other regarding the flawed American correctional system.

My eyesight fades and I begin to see white, a white room with old people, people telling stories of lives they have lived, stories that make this dream feel more real than my current life.

I awake to screams, a full-on domestic dispute. Zack is standing at the front door of the house, the screen doing a poor job of muffling the volume projecting itself into the face of his neighbour, who was standing on the other side of the door, afraid to enter the house with Zack's Doberman growling and baring its teeth at her. I rush up to mitigate the situation but am pushed back and hit the hardwood floor like the trees that made it up had fallen back in the 1990s. From my defeated position, I can see a half-snorted line of cocaine strewn across the homely table that provides the only indication in the room that this house wants to be called a home. Zack is high as hellfire and drunk as an entire generation of misguided misfit youth at a skate park. My gaze traces the room for a potential escape route, and I find myself sprawling to grab my clothing and stuff it in an old gym bag and ram my surfboards into my surf bag. I sprint through the language spewing from Zack's mouth like a gushing waterfall of garbage. His words are as polluted as the Pacific Geyser, and I can smell the toxicity with every *cunt* and *fuck* leaving his ungoverned lips.

"Where the fuck do you think you're going, you faggot! You owe me money!"

His eyes and words target my footsteps as they advance towards the side door.

"Dude, I don't owe you, I paid you rent and shit and I've only been here three weeks. I'm out, I can't—"

He runs across the room and picks up a knife that has been resting against a surfboard, once used for a rough ding repair and now as a weapon.

"You fucking owe me, your money hasn't done SHIT! You haven't done SHIT! You fucking cheap ass!" His anger is boiling to a place hotter than the seventh level of hell. He advances, knife in hand, and swipes the air in front of my face. Using this distraction, Zack's neighbour escapes the situation, and I hope she will call the police; but this is Makaha, and most people don't call the police in Makaha.

"Man, you need to relax, you don't want to do this." When he doesn't respond, I ask, "How much money do you want?"

"The damage has been done, you cheap ass!" he yells at me with no clarity in his mind to actualize the words dribbling out of his air sacks.

"I don't understand what you're upset about, but I'm going to leave, man, this is real fucked and I don't want to have any part of this. You're negative, man, and dangerous, every time we surf people say it, and you beat your dog when it doesn't listen, you yell at anyone doing anything you haven't asked them to do. Your mind is fucked, man, the drugs and shit, you're real fucked and you're ruining my vibe here!" I am spewing, as the Australians put it.

Zack freezes in his steps and throws the knife to the ground. For a moment I think that I have talked some sense into him, that maybe I can make this work and we will talk it out. And then the coffee table, now definitely not making the place a home, flies like an albatross off a cliff into the air — cocaine, bong, playing cards rolled into little cylinders, and loose change removing themselves from the grasp of gravity.

I sprint towards the porch door and throw my bags and boards over the deck railing, most likely putting dings in all my boards, one last piece of damage to the things that have made me more happy than if I were someone who paid three thousand dollars to find themselves at a Turtle Bay yoga retreat. To my surprise, no one follows as I look back and leap over the gate. I run into the empty street, I run until my legs can't hold me up anymore. And then I collapse, white beginning to surround me once again, accompanied by the sweet strings of a piano being strummed by a man in a tuxedo, boasting a smile as bright as that of Ray Charles.

ANICCA

If only this were a reality.

CHAPTER ?????????????

I step into that same dream again, the one that precluded my steps onto another flight from O'ahu to Big Island. The dream that Johnny disturbed, the dream that was facilitated by thirty thousand feet of dead air between the ocean and the molecules of my body, travelling at 700 miles per hour. The faces of men and women are around me, holding up writings and white glue–plastered photos pasted on the same construction paper you see in elementary schools to create airplanes you dream of flying inside one day. These albums describe their lives and the answers to the great questions asked by Gaugin's famous artwork; but I can't see the answers any more than I can see my own past, present, and future. I can see where they have all come from, I can see what they all are, but I cannot see where I am going.

"Ayden." A voice seeps into the myelin sheath of my brain, neurons firing, trying to organize and attribute this voice and its contents to some familiar sense of reality.

"Ayden, we have been waiting for you, we have been waiting for you to show us your life-album."

The voice is beginning to bother my exhausted neural pathways as they scatter and scan, attempting to actualize where the fuck I am. For the first time in or out of dream, I speak.

"What dream is this?" My lucidity is answered with a warm touch, a hand that promises the effects of Lorazepam mixed with one part whiskey and two parts psychological comfort.

"You are home, Ayden, it's okay." The voice projects itself onto the canvas of my mind, creating a rapid explosion of emotion coloured with the deepest shades of grey and hues of white. Confusion sets in.

"If I am okay, then tell me where the fuck I am."

The warm touch is turning into a clutch. I know this feeling on my shoulder. I know this hand: it is fear.

"He's lucid," I hear another voice proclaim.

"Let's begin," another chirps in like a bird expressing its excitement for spring.

"Ayden, we need to begin working on your photo album. What is your story?"

CHAPTER ???

My legs are bound in lactic acid, twisting and turning my body into a pretzel laced with the poison of anti-progression. The rain is pounding on my back as I look into the concrete floor for wisdom and wonder what the fuck just happened to me. I look behind me and see no one, just water all around me. The floor of the street begins to fill up like a graduated cylinder used in some biochemical experiment. Hercules and Zeus are holding me down as I push against the gods and make my way to my reef-tattered bare feet. I can feel the freshness of a reef cut on the base of my left foot between my arch and heel. It bites at me, preventing me from focusing on the loss of lucidity I had just experienced moments ago.

"I'll have it so that no one fucking lets you surf anywhere, brah! You fucking barney!"

A familiar voice. It's Zack, and for the moment I'm happy to hear his anger as it anchors me deep into this universe once more.

"I'll have it so that you're fucking wiped off of this island!"

166

I drag my surfboard and bags up from the ground and trudge through the streets until his voice is a domestic dispute put out by the distance of respite between us. I can see a convenience store and know that I need money but have no idea where I'm going. I walk across the freshly paved main strip and think of Johnny and what his departure has meant to my life. I can picture my bank statement, I can see the lack of zeros, and for the first time since arriving here I remove cash with the intent to leave this island forever.

"Ayden, are you listening? Come back."

CHAPTER ??

It's true what they say about paradise. Well, it's true what the wise say about it. It's not the palm trees, it's not the sand and sun—though these facets do help to sell the promise of pleasure when placed up against the backdrop of a highway in the middle of Alaska. I've seen this highway, well, a version of myself has seen that highway, and I hear about it as it persistently beats upon my temples like the notes of a detuned piano playing the same empty song of loss on repeat, like a forty-year-old bipolar trying to figure out life under the bridge of Fifth Avenue in Chicago. Yes, I've been there too. I can't decide if I'm speaking to the future me or a me from some years ago before arriving on this island. Where am I? Yes, paradise, it's a fucking sham in the material, tangible sense. Palm trees whither and sand is blasted from beaches in the blink of global climate change's eye— our very own self-induced, situational climate crisis. The point is, we always create or modify our surroundings so that only the weak eventually die off; we ensure it. We drown out different poverty levels by ensuring they consume until we, the maoi of America, stand looking down on them, smiles

168

enigmatic but secretly obvious and fashioned over years of perfectly tailored oppression.

The word *paradise* is within. I tell this to myself as the rain makes my bags heavy and my surfboards sag until their reflective cover is dragging in the mud along the banks of Makaha. Paradise is fucked. This is fucked, I tell myself continuously, a mantra of the mainland instilling itself on my dry palate, a dish best served with a bitter, fuck-life attitude. I not only can taste it, I start to believe it.

I look across the street for the bus, attempting to drag my sorry self off to Honolulu International with the hope of completing the mantra that is slowly weaving a web inside me like a spider with schizophrenia.

"No surfboards on the bus, brah. Sorry, get off."

"Fuck you. Seriously, just, fuck you."

It doesn't matter what job a Hawai'ian has, if you disrespect them like I just have, they will treat you to a taste of your own shit ice cream.

"Hey, brah? You wanna fucking walk with one leg? Fucking haole, go home, brah, we don' want no mainland bullshit here, off da bus, brah!"

The spider's web and the mantra are complete — fucked up, in disarray, and complete. My feet slug off into the mud and a tear treats my skin to a taste of lucidity. I've been here before — the tear on the face, but not this bus stop. I wish I had arrived at this bus stop earlier in life, but I haven't and I envy it. Through all the brutality that is contained in every drop of rain from my eye, I've missed this bus more than once. It's a good story, it's worth telling, it may even be worth living, so I take it; unknowingly until now, I take it and leave.

CHAPTER ????????

How I arrived back at Honolulu International is the combination of fact and fiction: a story I cannot tell for I cannot remember. Steel birds take shape across the sky as I stare out through the white blankets of rain that now pour from my eyes and out of my pores; I'm a living, breathing piece of hovering precipitation waiting to fall and ruin the world's day. I fall asleep on the airplane back to somewhere I can't remember. I fall asleep halfway through the ending of this story and forget how it ends. We are the sum of the feelings we get at the ending of everything we experience. We are loss; we are unfaltering sadness, complacency, momentary beliefs in happiness, amazement, frustration. We are the endings despite all the shit that has gone down before it. We are not the beginning or middle; we aren't even the plot line or setting. We are the finality of all experiences combined into one, and in our old age we feel every wrinkle on our bodies, these endings we physically embody and carry along with us as scars of good luck or bad.

I look into my withering hands, which may or may not remember the feeling of salt between them, the feeling of the ocean's currents, and I wonder if the teaming wrinkles were delivered to my body possibly by an emotion stronger than the realism of impermanence. I look unto my body for the answers of yesterday but still cannot fix the fact that I may or may not have felt as much difference and change in my life as this story's moral amplitude. Whoever's story it is, things have become hazy again, hazy like that nice story of Hawai'i. Though I think the ending was quite sad for that boy.

The benefits of selective memory loss, the benefits of the limits of science and the everlasting expansion of spirituality.

Paradise isn't a place, but I think I may have known it once.

PART III

CHAPTER ?

For most, 0400 is a time of rest, of replenishment,
a moment on the clock when the mind is reset and re-
energized for the coming day. For a man at war, it is the
time when metal meets flesh and when time — and all that
the common tongue knows to speak of it — becomes an
ethereal eternity cluttered with words once spoken and
words that failed to perch in their true form on the
doorstep of lips. For me, 0400 is the moment in my life
when I abandoned my country, the world of democracy,
and the girl back home who looks at the same picture as I,
adrift beside islands in the South Pacific, dodging bombs
headed for targets that few will ever know by name. Like
the ignition of a self-fulfilling idea, at 0400 I explore the
inches of the earth with a fire and rage that burns the stale
black of night and scorches the immotile light of day until
nothing is left but a man, a boat, and the mind of a
tarnished blank page in a photo album.

Up until the inception of the war movement, I had lived a life of leisure, internal prosperity, and love. Exploring the coastline of my Northern Oregon home with great wonder and excitement, I had no reason to think of foreign national powers, human rights violations, or genocide. It was a land I loved and a land that I would do anything to protect, for it was a sandbox of great wonder with no walls to create confines for the imagination. I had no care for the troubles in faraway lands; in fact, geography was the only subject I continually failed in grade school because of my lack of interest.

With hindsight, I now realize that every man, woman, and child says the same of the land they come from; it just is what it is, until the world is it at its doorstep with a match and a plan to take it away. But I was young and in love with the women, ocean, and earth that I came from, and nothing was going to take that from me. It was this attachment to something so many others in this world hold true that led me into the arms of hate, despair, and suffering on those nights in early October when I longed for the cold comfort of home.

I was sitting at a table listening to my favourite record when my brother, Adam, came into the room with a spark of excitement and angst in his step.

"Ayden! Ayden, we're going to war just like grandpa did, remember those stories he used to tell us about when the old radio crackled and he said that speech, you know, the president was all 'On this day, we go to war'? Remember that? Pretty nifty if you ask me!"

I look at him with an inquiring eye and a blank face. Adam always makes up stupid stories, and I'm currently failing my social studies class so I have no idea what the war is even about.

"Adam, you're such a dumbass, there's no war. Do you know what year it is? I'm heading over to Marielle's." He follows me out the door, the same jump still in his step, which was now serving as a sliver in the shadow of my easygoing life.

"Seriously! I'm not lying! Tell him, Ma!"

Our mother is walking up the steps in her grey dress, resembling the mood that is strewn across her vacant, expressionless face.

My mother is a caring woman and would do anything for anyone so long as the great Lord above would approve. In her religion she is faithful if not obsessed, yet in her vocalization of it she portrays elements of the deepest respect for diversity. I have never taken to this trait, often getting lost in the great Northern forests on Sundays and forgetting all about the will of God that is to be spoken in his house on that day. For me, the woods are my Sunday house and they have too much to offer in contrast to the words of some old wise man who tries to dictate how we live and what we do with our body parts. In all actuality, you could say that I have begun to establish somewhat of an agnostic persona, even to the point where my own mother doesn't even try to tear me away from the ocean's waves or the treetops that surround our home in Seaside when it comes to Sunday Mass. That is the brilliantly under-recognized trait my mother has: she cares for her God until it comes into conflict with someone else's. She might be considered quite the secularist if not for her absolute devotion to the Lord's word when it comes to socializing with other Catholics. She is a woman of faith and a woman of compassion and openness, and she is the one person I never feel compelled to explain myself to.

"Adam, run along back into the house," Mum says to my brother, who is already doing circles in the foyer, arms stretched out like an airplane and making gunfire noises. "Ayden and I need to chat."

"I told you, Ayden! It's true!" he yelps as he is pushed along with a broom into the salt-weathered, half-opened door and squeezes his body through the broken screen I was supposed to fix months ago.

Mum looks at me with a weary heart on her sleeve and a tear as salty as a sublimated ocean specimen on the cusp of her eye, the place where tears form and eventually break through, offering an open invitation to the flood waters of suffering to anyone within a hundred miles. I often do my best to talk that tear back into her eye, as if I could hold back the suffering if only I were to be able to talk it out of falling down her face and through the air that stands between us, down into the darkest of galaxies that exist beyond human understanding.

There is no stopping the tears of war, the tears that fall for so many reasons at the same time. Humans creating suffering for other humans until the result is a homeostatic condition where all the tears in the universe have been cried and one side says *I'm all out*. These are the tears falling now: war tears, blood-infused tears.

"Oh, Ayden, your grandfather has told me so many stories, I just, I can't let you go." She is now crying with her entire heart, there is no talking anything back inside her.

"Mum, just stop crying, I'll be fine, I won't have to go. It's a draft or something, all right?" I speak with the rhetoric of a grade eight social studies student, yet I have the knowledge in my heart of a political science professor.

"Mr. Mortenson asked me to tell you that there is a mandatory meeting at the town hall tonight. I, I don't know what they will be doing or saying but it's important, so you go. You go and let me know what we can do to get you out of this." Another tear breaks free from the confines of her eye and traces a path down her face, a trail that will be travelled many more times before my story comes to close, the denouement of my life, though at this moment my soul is telling me that I have already reached that point.

At the beginnings of war, there is a flicker of excitement. Even in those who are completely against it in every way, shape, or form, this little light grows when it meets up with others who have that spark, and eventually, you have an entire nation that is burning as strong as the fires of hell. My flame is dormant, snuffed out by my anxiety, something that I am not used to on these shores; it has been stolen by the dark woods of my home, the fresh scent of my morning air, the taste of my young lover's lips, and the waves that do the same thing for me every time I paddle out into them.

I pull up to the beach with my wetsuit and surfboard hanging from the roof rack of my Jeep. It is early October and Seaside Point is firing on all cylinders. It is the kind of day when your heart starts to beat even before you jump into the current and struggle your way out; by all standards, it is another epic day of lefts to be had.

"Yo, bro, you hear about this war?" my friend John says. "We going to war, man, fucking wiiild!

New countries, new breaks, new girls, can you imagine, bro? We gonna get good at surfing." My spark becomes a flame if for no other reason than the mention of foreign waves, which I cannot afford on my bowling alley budget.

"Yeah, man, my mum was going on about it, crying and stuff, religions got her praying right now, probably." I find myself laughing at the woman who has only one intention: to care. War has a way of bending our minds into thinking that anyone who opposes is somehow "not cool," at the very least. War is a plague, and most dangerously, it can become a childish popularity contest.

"Ah ha! Shit, man. Well, whatever—we get to leave the rules and shit behind here in this shunt of a town and travel the world, what the fuck do we care?"

John is an only child from a family that would be considered wealthy by the Queen's standards. His father is a drunk and an engineer, in that order, and his mother is an Associate Justice for the Supreme Court who works out of Salem for the majority of the week. This leaves John and his father to fight out their differences in her absence, which often shapes the relationship he has with his mother on the weekends. It is, in all physical form, the American nuclear family; indeed, there is something nuclear about it.

John has a darker complexion, but no one knows where in his bloodline his genetics were influenced in this way. He is an American-born child, through and through, with the temper of a megalomaniac and a laugh as rich as Swiss chocolate. His brown eyes can burn a hole in any blanket and can melt the heart of any big-city girl who happens to pass through our small coastal town. Our relationship runs deep, and the cuts we give each other often run deeper. But it is this relationship that follows us and gives us strength when we are forced with the decision to join death and to deal with the aftermath of our decisions.

We paddle out into the foggy wonderland that is our home surf break, duck-diving waves that may soon become bullets and mortar fire. We begin sliding weightlessly down the faces of the ocean as easily as aircraft cut through air. It is the last time John and I will surf together and the last time I will ever see John the easygoing, carefree troublemaker and proud surfer.

I leave the water with my arms heavy and legs as weak as a jar of homemade jelly; it is the best and strongest I will feel for some time to come. Looking across the parking lot, I see John — captain of the untamed sea, student of the untamed world — and I try to understand to some finite point where war has buried its treacherous trick down in the confines of his heart. The war flames he has instilled in me begin to blend with the fear, anguish, and anxiety that can kill a man in a war as quickly as when pin strikes gunpowder. I strap my short board on top of my gun, a board most commonly used in bigger surf, and fire up my Jeep, slamming the gas pedal down to keep the air pumping and mixing with the gasoline as the vehicle idles. The air runs cold in my hair, and I take my bangs in my mouth and suck the salt from them, bending my head to the left as the excess water in my system drains out my nose and onto the steel floor at my feet. My

180

headlights illuminate waves that will be open to play in under the full moon at the end of the month.

If I make it until then.

CHAPTER ??

The town hall is bustling with little sparks bumping into one another and beginning to spread the wages of war like wildfire. I can see John as he enters the room in his faded rolled-up jeans and singlet, both of which are wet with the ocean. His dark complexion always stands out when he enters a room, and his white teeth, compliments of the justice system, always beam like pearls at the bottom of the darkest waters.

"So, you sign up yet or what?" he asks. "Let's do this, man. What do we choose, air force? Shoot some motherfuckers down? Or you wanna get into the guts and grit, man, real war-style, and stick a bayonet into these cowards?" He is speaking as John always speaks about anything he is excited about: full-on and stoke-filled. His energy bounces off the walls that display and reinforce Uncle Sam and the American Army's strongest weapon. His energy is doing Uncle Sam's work.

"Ladies and gentlemen," a booming voice rings out over the hall PA like the last words spoken by God, although my mother didn't know them. "We are gathered here today, on this great American soil, as I speak through this free American air, to tell you that we are at war." The man's voice gives strength to his cause. His chest puffs out proudly, displaying medals of wars that have already come to pass. His mustache holds strong and dark over the conviction of his words. His height speaks in opposition to his thick legs, which have surely run trenches and support arms that have dragged bodies across the bloodiest of farmers' fields.

I peer down at my own legs, hands, and arms, noticing that I am a child in the shadow of a great warrior. I feel alone.

"The air will no longer be free and the soil beneath your feet will no longer be yours if we do not stand up against this great, foreboding terror. Communism and the great plague of red flows like crimson blood down our wells and into the drinking water of our families and the water of generations to come. We will stand, we will fight, and we will prevail as the great American idea always has. We are Americans: we spill red blood for the Lord and reap in the prospect of a sun that shines the colours of America. For this great country will not succumb to the threat of an ill-minded sun nor the intentions of a dictator who holds within his mind and heart the blasphemous ideology of a world led by terror and threat. Our minds will fight his intention and our bodies will act as vessels to carry out a swift and powerful surge against the great red terror in the name and hope of keeping our wells free of this poison and of keeping the future generations of America free of plight!" The crowd roars, which pleases the great leader's mustache, its fibres turning

183

upright as the sickening smile of war spreads across his face.

I stand in a moment of uneasiness, my heart beating harder than it ever has while out chasing double-overhead waves at the point. Cheers rise up around me, cheers that will soon be manufactured and tailored into bloody war cries, calling out strategized orders. Cheers that will soon be replaced with a mother's cry as time grows on and the days in faraway places grow dark with malice. I want to turn around and run out the door, run away from this man and his medals, his strong body, and his indoctrinating tongue. I am slowly becoming what wartime America considers an enemy of the cause; my mind is fighting back, and it is only a matter of time before my body will begin to do the same.

The room is the typical wood-panelled gymnasium that adults only see at election time. To them, this room is political in nature and thus a natural environment for this speech to be held in. To me, it is the free-throw line, the top of the key, the lines that are sticky from cola spilt across them in the dark during high school dances. It is hardwood made soft by the treading footsteps of momentary crushes of high school love and slow dancing. The lights are the witnesses to many a first high school kiss, and the air is no stranger to high school band music notes and vocal tones that the church attempts to ban year after year. All of this is being overlooked for nothing but the simple fact that some man in some fucked-up country wants to kiss our high school dates at our high school dances, moving to our high school music while spilling American cola across the hardwood floor just like we Americans do.

I turn around without acknowledging John or the war and slip out of the room with stealth like elegance. I would be good at war.

The road emits the fresh smell of fall as the rain above slowly begins to drift further into interior America in blissful, apocalyptic fashion. Like battle, the weather will soon spread from the coast inwards over the land, the land I should be protecting, the land that would be taken by fire instead of water if everyone were to act in the same opposition I am posturing. The trees hang solemnly over the street, momentarily blocking out the street lamps as the wind tosses and turns their leaves as naturally as human evolution.

I can see the crest of a wave break out over the cliff edge as I walk up the ridge around the point where John and I once shared the same belief system about this life and what we want from it. I sit down where the ocean meets the land and take the cold spray on my face as a refreshing break from the words of Mr. Mustache. Sitting, staring out with catatonic intention, I imagine and dream hard, ignoring the water seeping through my navy knitted sweater and the cold permeating my skin like acid on flesh. The moon holds my attention and I have to make a move — conscription is a finality, and not only will I be taken from what I love but I will be ridiculed and exiled during training for leaving and not formally accepting my duties from the map maker tonight. I have nowhere to turn but to the place that has always given me the answer, a place that has always offered refuge to not only myself but also to generations that had come to pass. The ocean grins at me, its waves grinding against reef, inviting me and warning me of the dangers that lay ahead if I choose her over war. There is the opportunity for a conformed fight against the spilling of my blood, or there is the great unknown of rigging up a vessel and tacking out into the dark depths of a world less discovered, a place where I can hide from terror rather than fight it. I gather my mind off the sharp, slippery, sea-infused rocks, hold it back in place, and begin my walk home under the darkening sky, uncertain of what is to come but firm in my epiphany that this is truly the only way to keep from harming myself and others in this world.

***

The morning grows over my bed as it breaks the confines of frost from my windowsill. I can smell the rich scent of eggs, bacon, and pancakes as they grow rigid against the grill downstairs. My room is a clutter of old surf magazines and maps of the Pacific Northwest coastline, instruments I use to chart potential undiscovered surf breaks in the area. I stole them from the University in Portland along with a lengthy list of topographic maps of the ocean floor. These are my side arms, and I believe they will complement my artillery nicely as I fight the loneliness and dark, deep sacrifice that I will make of my pride.

I stumble across my room and into the hallway on legs drunk with the fear and excitement of my plan to escape on whatever seaworthy boat I can find. In the back of my plan is the sacrifice of losing my family, and this stumbles down the stairs with me as sorrows often do before one steps onto the battlefield. Adam is already seated at the table with his favourite comic book propped up against the cereal box, a perfect image of himself sixty years from now. I am not going to fight for his life. This thought passes through me with a jolt of hatred for my self-fulfilling cause. I push it down, deep into a place where I allow intellect and survival to govern my emotions like a skipper lost in an ocean filled with double-edged shark teeth. With a balancing act of survival and attachment, I cross the kitchen floor and sit down beside the boy I can only hope will become a man in my absence from the great American surge on misunderstanding and political difference.

"Eggs, honey?" Mum is standing across the kitchen with a ladle in hand, displaying a look of absence on her face. It is as though she has locked her emotional crisis in the cellar and left it for some kids to find when they smoke pot in this abandoned old post-war home. It is a horror story in the making.

"Sure, thanks, Mum. I, uh, I appreciate you making breakfast." My voice trips on my lips like a child who has been given a candy behind his mother's back. She stares into my thoughts like mothers do, with concern and wisdom far beyond the current human understanding of love. As the last sliver of homemade cooking makes its way into my word-parched mouth, I fight the urge to tell my plan, extinguishing one worry while creating another in my family. Luckily the moment breaks free from its frozen tundra as the door swings open.

The rear porch of the house always has the most sun in the morning and is often my main entrance to the house as I am always outback building and digging into the earth in search of answers. Marielle bursts through this door and hugs me harder than she ever has before. The truth of it is, we are on the outs and these hugs have never been the norm. I have planned a surf trip for the following year that will take me across the world to Indonesia, and neither of our young hearts can take the pressure of such a dream's existence. At this moment in my life, nothing in the world draws the love out of me like the ocean, yet in this one moment, knowing that I will be eloping with the ocean in a matter of hours, I feel for her, I long for her, and I long for humanity and its touch.

"Ayden, I heard you ran out last night," Marielle says. "Everyone…well, everyone is talking about it and saying you left town. Are you going to sign up today? You know they're looking for you — not just John, who is pretty pissed, I've gotta say — but also that big guy with the mustache, you know? The hero? Are you going to be one of those for me? He was saying, you know, that your actions now will govern the rest of your life — who you are and who you will be known as."

I can see where she stands: in the smack fucking middle trenches of the republican dogma that is slowly clouding the skies of my perfect little beachfront town.

"Yeah, I'll be going over today, is that guy coming here?" I ask with a hesitation that undeniably proves that my words are thick with deceit. But no one questions me on the grounds that everyone is shit-scared of what will happen if I really do plan to fuck off.

"Ayden, they're pretty pissed," she says. "There's been a lot of draft dodgers in California over the past few weeks, there's a lot of fire out for the gutless pussies like them, you know? Let's go find him and sort this out."

Before I can interject, my arm is leading my body out the back door and into the green field that has held my body afloat since I can remember. The grass feels soft on my feet, I can feel myself floating as the blood in my veins fills up with the response of flight. I want to drift up into the clouds, I want to push her away and tell her that she is a fucking puppet and that her love is plastic coated; I want to do anything but be her hero, this country's pawn. In times of political adversity and war, women are the gasoline to a man's spark, but Marielle is made of water and I am drowning.

The ground rises up beneath me like burning bullets on the sand, turning the soles of my feet to pins and needles as the grass turns to sand and the sand to glass. Everything in me wants to run, my very existence wants to escape the chronic needles that tear into my skin like an open wound exposed to the winter months of time.

"Yeah, Marielle, fuck. Like I said, I'll do what I have to." My words are drawn on a fifth-grade blackboard and my palms are awaiting a sure smack from Marielle's ruler.

"You don't have to be such an asshole. I'm just here to let you know because I don't want people to think you're one of those hippie pussies."

"And what if I am? What if I am, Marielle? A fucking hippie pussy who is against this dogma, this bullshit, this crusade? Fuck, you have no idea. Where's your gun! Where's your gun, Marielle!" She knows my plan, it was written in brackets between

189

every word that shamelessly gushed from my treasonous mouth.

It is time to run.

Marielle runs across the backyard, ignoring the feeling of the soft, sweet comforting grass spreading itself between her toes like soft clouds filling the spaces between blue skies. Her hair floats behind her like the tail of a jet stream and I can no longer see her face, but she runs like a true soldier to spread the word that the man she apparently loves and will do anything for needs to be bound and burnt on the cross. The world will soon know that Ayden has a plan to leave this parcel of land on a small boat, out into the blue, black, and unknown. A true sailor of my own ignorant sea, and all I need now is a vessel with a heart as seaworthy as my own.

I take every moment I can to appreciate the land under my feet as the angels over America ring out the brilliance of a million softly spoken words with every breath I draw into my lungs. I gather up a laundry basket full of supplies from the kitchen and a backpack filled with maps that I am only slightly familiar with using. The lump of clothing under my bed will now be my only reminder of home as I stuff it into a travel surf bag, huddled in with my board and ten sticks of Sex Wax. My mind is a stuffed animal as I rush a note to my mother and friends. There are no words in the dictionary of any language that would please and give respite to the American dreams I am about to shatter like the impact of the earth's oceans on American soil. I will now become a part of the world out there and more so of the world inside my future self. Two days ago stealing a sailboat from the marina was a thought that would put me into distress. Today, it's like packing a stick of gum next to my socks in a waterproof bag.

My life lay out before me on the floor at my feet:

- 1 international marine guide
- 5 pairs of wool socks
- 2 pairs of briefs
- 5 pairs of board shorts
- 2 pairs of jeans
- A mix of Nautical charts (some missing pages)
- A compass
- 1 surfboard, bag, and fins
- 2 wetsuits
- Enough food to last 3–4 weeks
- A heart with the intention of finding a new world

CHAPTER ?

My Jeep roars louder than I'd like. It is 4:30 a.m. on a Sunday, and word has already begun to spread of my intentions; no one knows how I plan to avoid the draft, and most figure that it is impossible and only hearsay. My mother assured the community in her soft, catholic way that rumours will be rumours, but the sound of my engine on this dimly lit and damp doomsday on an October morning speaks in a different tongue. My headlights burn the air in front of me as the eyes of a racoon stare out from the side of the highway. For a brief moment, I think about his home and how it might be destroyed by war, and then I remind myself of the artistry behind the thought and the reality behind lead and gun powder.

My foot hits the accelerator harder as I smash through the marina gates, and I hit my brakes just short of the docks. A boat I've known since I've had eyes rocks smoothly back and forth against its protective side bumpers. Standing before me is my key to the western ocean, to the South Pacific, to the possibility of anything at the hands of some god; if there is one, I will soon find out. Her ropes reach up

into the night sky and her bow beckons to the ocean
like an eagle perched on a cliff gesturing to the sky in
front of it. The pearl-white gel coat reflects the oceans
waves as they dance their way up her hull, brushing
softly, ever so smoothly coaxing her out into blue,
out into the useless unknown, a uselessness that only
surfers and sailors are akin to. She is my Uncle
Richard's boat and my vessel of the night. Not privy
to his whereabouts for some months now, I assure
myself I will have at least a two-day head start before
they realize how I managed to leave the stars and
stripes behind. I grip my basket of gear, and with my
surf bag slung over my shoulder, I hobble like a
strongman competitor to the finish line—my uncle's
boat, the *Moana*.

I grip the bowline, throw my gear on board,
then jump on and tuck my rations below deck. I
smash the lock to the cabin with an onboard hatchet
and welcome myself to my new home. Letters that
look like building permits and zoning documents are
tossed about. My uncle is a wealthy investor and a
real estate agent, both professions that afford him the
ability to put a mere fifteen-dollar lock on a fifty-
thousand-dollar boat. There's enough headroom to
walk around upright, and a tiny kitchen is set across
from a bed. Up at the far end is another cubby with a
second bed, which my uncle often called the *Oh shit*
bed—the one where you batten down the hatches
and hope for the best when strong squalls challenge
you to the death. I give my new apartment the once
over and find some canned food and pasta in the
cupboard—more than most can say about their first
home at my age. I crawl out of the cabin and
scramble across the deck. I begin the routine check

my uncle taught me, ensuring that all the rigging and sails are fit for departure.

- Hackline – Check
- Rigging knives – Check
- Scanners set for channels 13, 14, and 16 - Check
- Short-wave radio receiver – Check
- Lifesling and tackle – Check
- Mirror for signalling – Check, but most likely not of use
- Channel-lock pliers – Check
- Whipping twine – Check
- Log book, tide tables, knotstick, protractor, lead line, pencil, eraser – Check, check, check

My head on a swivel, drifting back and forth between the boat's upper deck and lower locker, I notice a flicker of light to the left of the boat as a voice comes booming out through the false security that my checklist had created.

"Hey! Who's there, hay?"

It was a deep Australian voice, probably the dock master. This is the man you want to add to your checklist, let him know your route and bearing, but instead I am fighting to avoid a sure lifeline if things go wrong.

I dodge about onboard as his steps grow closer, grow more challenging to my plot. He has a large mag light and shows little to no hesitation to use it to bash my head in. He scuttles about, checking boats with his light before noticing my Jeep at the end of the dock. Just as his gaze finds my Jeep, I jump into the water, immediately stealing his attention. He didn't see which boat I jumped from but is frantically searching the silky wet surface for some form of life.

"I'll get you, ya cunt! Where you at? Where you at? I'ma get you, ya cunt!" He could destroy me before the police could read me my rights, and this is his sole intention. I use all my paddle power to fight the swirling current under the docks that push and pull at my perfectly deteriorating plan. My clothing weighs down on me as I block my ears to the man's voice and wretch and rip at my muscles as if escaping the grasps of some enemy attempting to strap me to my deathbed in the middle of some South Pacific island jungle. I scurry up the beach on a shoreline that feels like a bullet-riddled beach landing and scrape my knees and legs up rocks that tear into my layers of flesh like fresh blades of steel grass, grass so unlike the kind in my backyard. I drag blood up the rocks, and the salt from high tide burns deeper and deeper into my nervous system as I rub against the salt-drenched logs and bull kelp. My Jeep stands there in the dark and I lunge myself into the front seat as if I'm the last soldier to escape alive in some raid gone wrong.

I slam my Jeep into reverse and it roars into the night, one fog light out from smashing into the gate. I have left behind only one clue. I tear back down the dark highway to Marielle's house, praying the dock master hasn't called the police or checked my uncle's boat.

The air has lost all stillness and is now pacing around my every step, waiting for me to fuck up and crash into any situation that presents itself. I move farther and farther back in a direction I know I will be leaving behind for good. I roll up to Marielle's backyard and put my Jeep in park, pulling back hard on the parking break as if for the last time that it would ever be driven. I grab my longboard from the trunk and ride off into the night, leaving my one last symbol of the American dream parked inside a cavern of woods that would devour the car until daybreak, at which time the police would contact my mother and the witch hunt for Ayden Wallace would begin. The concrete feels smooth beneath the wheels of my longboard, a motion I will not feel again for quite some time.

As I roll up to the dock only the ocean stands before me, welcoming me with open arms into a home I have only been a casual guest in up until today. As if the incident one hour ago were a dream, I grab the final line and toss it into the past. By now, the dock master has most likely finished his bottle of Jim Beam and passed out in the office as he had often done after he chased us from the docks when we were young.

Sureness rises up in me as if I have just finished serving my first victory at war. I start the outboard motor and ferry myself out into the black horizon, which gives way to blue as the land mass of home behind me is swiftly swallowed up by the biggest decision of my life.

CHAPTER ??

Those who possess private beaches only in their minds are far closer to enlightenment than those with the means to purchase them in their physical form. I think deeply about the favourite places of my childhood and try hard to focus on the moments when I have felt I needed to see and explore new lands. The thought fails and I long for a private beach; maybe if I could afford one of those, I could hide away from all the hurt, the emotional wrenching in my gut, and the need to force the Buddhist fundamentals of nonattachment upon the rock that I am, stuck in the side of a mountain of attachments. I think of all those friends I grew up with who are from wealth and who are now in post-secondary institutions, learning about the feelings in my life through the lens of psychology or some other social science–related discipline. *The Psychosocialspiritual Facets Associated with Draft Dodging.* I can see the headline just above the rising lines of the sun as I turn off the motor and begin to haul up the main sail for the first time of many.

Growing up, I was always fond of sailing, joining my uncle on his short but adventurous journeys down into central California, which was a regular occurrence over the midsummer days. Sailing taught me to fly; it taught me of the ocean's temperament, which soon led me to building my life around it and living within it. Only the ocean would dare snuff out the flames of war, absorb the bullets of Normandy, and continue to control who receives the spoils of battle. Through sailing, I learned of the natural order of things and how everything we do, no matter how small or large, is relative to the ocean's emotions and her ability to transform the shoreline and the fate of us all in some way or another.

The main sail is luffing up above me as the wind pressures itself against the boat and begins to push us hard and fast with the all-too-familiar gesture of letting us know who is the captain of who. I trim the mainsheet in hard and set my bearings due west into the vast shades of blue. The boat skips over the swell lines and plummets deep and hard into the troughs of the water, giving way to the salty sweet spray of freedom, splashing up and into the dark holes of my eyes. The offshore winds, which are so rare to the area, are steady and strong, speeding us along on a broad reach and oddly aiding my crusade.

Looking over my shoulder as does an owl searching out food at night, I continue to anticipate the coast guard rushing up on my heels with a motorized fury, waiting not only to send me to war but also to throw me in jail for grand larceny and draft evasion. The shoreline behind me is distant, dissipating from my sight but not from my consciousness. A fear within me dwells deep in the realization that I am actually scared that no one is chasing after me, that this pilgrimage may indeed be my own destiny — my personal legend as summoned by Uncle Sam's angry mother, one that may progress from conceptualization into a tangible and existential roller coaster with no start and no finish. I could never have known how true this was when I stole this boat and left the land I love. I tell myself that the land of freedom and opportunity has ceased to be so, and in this I give myself to the ocean and her perpetual offerings, which no governed land mass in this world can or will ever be able to offer in its totality: peace.

I pass the outer islands I had dreamt of surfing while growing upwards and outwards from the freedom-blunting school chair that held my body captive for so many perfect swells as a kid. I had told myself that my mother was right when she said to stay in school, get a good job, surf perfect waves every winter, and then repeat. Nothing could be further from my current reality. I can paddle out to my favourite barrelling slab and surf it, but today there is something else on my plate and in my mind's face. I am in battle as I fight over the swell, smashing up and down, up and down, up and down. I have sailed in rough waters before on trips up the coast to Neah Bay in Washington and around into Canada, when I discovered a land where freedom and free enterprise isn't just a label on the back side of a pickle jar marked with *Made Somewhere Else*. I thought about the possibilities up in the vast land of Canada where there lay perfect, unsurfed reef breaks only accessible by boat and a courage spoken by the mouths of war heroes. I look back and no longer see the shoreline — I am what sailors and surfers alike call home.

I know the sail up to Vancouver Island will be rough this time of year as I'll be battling not only the current but also the rough north westerlies that hammer the ocean's face like a tornado in a child's sand box. I reach down and pull the mainsail in hard to crease out any luffing and head below decks with my bearing set and my stomach screaming for food. And so it is I have my first meal at sea. I don't pray, for God has turned from me, I don't wish or expect anything but the worst. Through this I find strength and the will to survive at the bottom of a can of brown beans and off the bones of the sea.

I hide below deck and fight the urge to remain here forever. I have sailed long and hard oceans, but I have never sailed against the will of God and country. I check my bearings as my compass bobs around in the clear, jelly-like solution, turning and tossing to balance itself in the violence of an oncoming storm. I'm overdue for respite, for a reprieve from my own mind that twists and torments my soul like a clock that refuses to stop reminding the world that its hands have been there before, eliciting the same ticking result every second after second. I think of the moai carved by the Rapa Nui on Easter Island as my social studies teacher taught me back when a pencil was the only weapon my country required me to use against my will. I think of their existence as a reminder of wars come to pass, wars I have not witnessed but have lived through indirectly, brought up inside the same nursery that fosters the stars and stripes that fall with the

200

imperialistic grace of a thousand doves leaping into the sky above Ypres, only to be shot down by the next of kin to the fallen. The mothers feed but do not foster change in these children of the West.

CHAPTER ??

"Mr. Wallace, what is your answer to number six?" I had drifted off again into the waves.

"Ma'am, number six is the same as seven." I offered my guess with cheek.

"And that would be…?"

"Well, I got six wrong, so, not that," I said, laughing out loud in hopes that any of the three girls in the front row of class would rejoice in my humour, and they did. She looked back at me with soft and youthful eyes, the kind of eyes that are not only trying to avoid the ill will of man but also to altogether believe that he is capable of peace. I smiled, an honest gesture in return for her reassurance that being the class clown was still in style in 1938. She had made me feel this free and lost for words before. Her name was Marielle, and her intention would be to make me into a man worth missing while at war, and a man away she had made me. I think of her skin as it brushed against me for the first time, her lips that made me go home and masturbate for a week straight. Through all the salt in the ocean I can taste her perfume on my lips and

202

smell the sweetest indoctrinated angel I ever laid nose on.

That was then and this is now: a boat, a boy, and a heart shit-scared of country, house, and home. I struggle against my ever-growing great depression, which has begun before the war has even ended. My arms are rubbed down with plastic cement and polyester resin, cemented and glassed against the sides of the boat. My feet are covered in four-ounce fibreglass cloth and the polyester hot coat is solidifying my position deep within the bowels of the boat's hull. In all respects, I have become trapped within my vessel, my escape plan. I look to the ceiling, where I see old drawings, hand drawn by some boy younger than I in a different time and place. Drawings that I surely would have sketched myself and sent up to Marielle in the first row of math or biology class — she was always sitting in the front row, eager to learn about whatever America had decided was important for her to code and process within her mind for the rest of her days.

It's a cartoon displaying an island and a man with a large smile and stick, or shovel, or bottle of rum in hand, which he celebrates by arching it up into the air as if he has just found the fountain of youth. There is a palm tree behind his badly drawn body, the bark of it twisted like the chasms of the hull as they smash against the swell that is piercing the boat and surely engulfing the deck above my head. Oregon has palm trees, but it doesn't have this type of escapism. At least not at this point in the story, the point when the hands on some God's clock tick down rather than up to something. This is how I see things. This thought makes me feel alone, and the thought that I am seemingly the only one in my country who sees it this way makes me feel even more so.

The badly drawn image is my sanctuary, my glamour magazine or tabloid that promises a happier future. My eyes lose track of my own body and I become catatonic, transfixed on my little HB pencilled paradise, thinking of that day in class when Marielle laughed at my jokes, that day our lips locked, and that day when her heart fell for the gun, bayonetting mine into the scorched earth. This image does not hold back its brutality, blood plastered and accurate with my eyes closed; the image of my paradise filling itself with crimson blood, staining the palms of trees and turning our lead character with the smile into a devil. Yes, that is surely a bottle of rum he is holding.

CHAPTER ??

Experts say that prolonged sleep and loss of appetite are related to major episodes of depression, adjustment disorders, and other psychological phenomena possibly connected with circumstantial or chemical changes in one's brain. I had lost the night to the day, and the day to the night. Forty-five days had passed without the sight of light beyond the rising of the sun's face growing across my lap through the small cabin window, which continually begged me to break free from my mind and attend to the ocean. The weight of psychological fibreglass, now as solid as the finished gloss coat of a big-wave surfboard, pressed ruthlessly onto my chest. They say that every vessel needs a captain just like every body needs a mind to guide it through life. I had lost both and was deeper into the black than João Fernandes Lavrador in his final days of life.

João Fernandes Lavrador discovered Terra do Lavrador (what we now know as Greenland), a name which soon translated and translocated to its southern ancestor in Canada — that is, Labrador. His ending would see his royal patent of 1498 drown with him on a voyage to The New World, a world

205

that he had potentially attempted to find exile and refuge in—or maybe he was on a voyage that aided in the creation of strife and conflict; whichever way you look at his journey, it was mine. Lost to sea and surely fastened down by his past dealings with Moorish imprisonment and North African slave and gold trading, it is almost certain that his conclusion stumbled upon my own dismay at some point.

Nonetheless, there is one difference between our ancient mariner's journey and my own: He, like many conquistadors, fought and conquered for country and home; I am abandoning mine. He was celebrated; I am shamed. If it was exile he was seeking, it was to be drawn someday by an HB pencil with a smile and flag in his hand as he retired with congruent leaps and bounds of joy. The image that stares deep into my waking eyes is blood and loss, and I am the one avoiding war. I have been sailing on a bearing that I have forgotten and I have been feeling an ocean that has offered me no mercy. With the uneasy emotion of stillness, I roll my coagulated legs out of the small loft bed and feel the splinters of the deck rub their way into the soles of my bare feet. The compass bobs in the jelly like a dead fish suspended in the black sea. I stretch my tingling fingers across the inside of the hull and reach towards the deck latch, winding back the lever and snapping open the lock, my civil defence mechanism popping open and revealing a light that scalds my dilated pupils, searing the colours from my irises. I falter my way up the four-step ladder and taste the notion that I may experience freedom or I may experience certain death, pending the current condition of my vessel, my lifeline, and the sun's effect on my mentality.

It's a curious thing, putting your entire life in the hands of some fibreglass, steel, and rope, for the ocean is surely potential apocalypse in the right conditions. Thousands of years after the great explorers of late, after our great hero and voyager João Fernandes Lavrador drowned at sea, humans are still following suit. It is as though some of us are drawn to the ocean and take full sanctuary in knowing that it someday may be the only one to offer us a pure finality. Like a human draining the chemicals from the business end of a cigarette, we claim that at least we know how we will die. I wonder, as I trace my hands around the pearling white port and starboard gel-coated sides of the boat, if my friend on the ceiling below deck thinks like me. It's amazing the punishment a boat can handle when faced with swell and how little it can stand when breached by foreign objects. Like a fish force-fed land instead of water, a boat's hull is only capable of dealing with two elements and is surely destroyed if faced with the others. Like flesh to steel or fire, we are of water and contain properties the same. My punishment is a concurrent existence.

The stern of the boat balanced as a teeter-totter would if two children of equal weight had tried to sit face to face in love, both refusing to take the first leap and push the teeter-totter down to the ground for fear of damaging the other end. A perfect balance of disaster waiting to happen, potential energy at its finest and worst. Young love like this is a stalemate, and we learn that something always gives — something always has to give — in love and war.

The water is warmer, and I realize that between feeding myself rations of canned tuna and water to stay alive for the past forty-five days, I have landed somewhere other than where I intended. My depression had given autonomy to my boat to sway in the ocean's currents and the sky's winds, allowing nature to dictate my path. True chaos theory at its finest, perhaps.

CHAPTER ???????

Forty-five days lost or forty-five days gained? It's hard to determine your level of optimism when in crisis and fleeing war at sea. The boat has run a wreck on a slab of dry reef that I am sure will someday produce good to all-time surf pending the right swell direction and conditions. The reef stretches its lava fingers deep into the lagoon of an island of the type I have only ever seen in surf magazines. Pipeline, Off-The-Wall—these are the reef fingers I have seen in photos, which feel like accessible memories.

I scurry down into the cabin that once encapsulated my fragile mind like a car weaved inside the twisting vortex of a hurricane. Enough rations left to potentially catch me some dinner, but there's no way it'll last me long enough to survive the week. Waves batter the side of my once-brilliant galleon and the floor panels fill with water so salty that anything metallic is already beginning to experience the effects of oxidization.

My body is beginning to feel the effects of a very similar nature, my knees weak and clunky, my arms hinged upon failing joints and overstretched, protein-diminished muscle. I look around for a bag and catch a green, red, and blue rucksack and tether it to my waist. I look under the bed, which is now beginning to float up like Jesus resurrected — flat and limp and gradually inching its way softly towards the ceiling of its world. I look up and notice my HB drawing, my portrait of happiness, as water falls into my eyes and creates a depressing foreshadow that is cast across my vision and my image of a perfect sundown. An image that once demanded a catatonic state of seduction is now a momentary flash of light at sunset that children try to see from airplane windows and on faraway tropical islands. The image sinks as I pull my rucksack and my limited supplies above deck.

Despite the catastrophe and perfect storm below deck, my eyes touch warm sunlight as I reach my way into day. The aftermath of a storm continues to pressure the hull, and I fashion a lifeboat out of the five life jackets luckily attached to the bow locker of the boat in preparation for this chapter of my life. I will return to the ship and obtain remaining materials later, knowing that for my own mental stability I need to plant my toes on formal dirt. I tether the life jackets and place a piece of board over top of them, and only once I jump into the ocean with the grace of a surfer disembarking a surf charter in the Mentawais for the first time do I notice how out of my element I am. The jackets sprawl out north, south, east, and west, creating a compass bearing that points to soaking-wet catastrophe. I begin to kick and paddle, attempting to avoid the dry reef patches that swirl with malcontent and try to suck me deep into the spiny fingers of some foreign urchin that most likely contains, at the very least, a strong bout of anxiety for the next five days, making any human stare at their wounds until believing that death is certainly upon them.

Survival is a mental game, we all know that, or at least we hear it, and a fight with fire coral, a provoked bull shark, or a box jelly fish all equate to the trials and tribulations of a full-blown mental blitzkrieg of defeating thoughts. The silent death of the sea is lonesome, creating doubt and mistrust in one's capacity to survive. Every kick and stroke away from the fingers of reef remind me of this, though I know it is inevitable that I will smash my knuckles as I have done so many times before while surfing shallow reef breaks. I look down into the water and through the intoxication of adrenalin rising in my bloodstream; I notice a shark-enticing blood trail surrounding my body. When you see a shark fin while surfing, you catch a wave and paddle in; when you see a fin while on a makeshift life raft, you panic and spread your blood into the water faster than a flash flood in the outback of Australia.

My muscles seize and burn, partially from being stuck in one position for the last forty-five days and partially from the resistance of the current against my will. One, two, three shark fins — shoot a bullet at me, this is heavier than war. I jump to my feet and lurch across the sharp reef, feeling each precise incision taking place against my ankles and soles. "No. 10 blade" slice, "scalpel" slice — the ocean is treating me to a permanent form of surgery that is unwelcomed and unrequired. As each barnacle slices through the multiple layers of my epidermis, tearing fleshy layer by fleshy soft layer, the salt water creeps in, making volcanoes of pain all over the lower half of my body. I stumble and treat my hands to the volcano, slash, cut, stab, feel, life, now.

My body resembles a wounded soldier, my enemy left behind the inner reef—disgruntled and already planning their next attack. I pass out into the warm sand and feel white air wash over me.

"Ayden, can you hear us? Are you with us? Let's paint a picture, it appears that this moment is important to you. It could be real! It could be relevant!"

I blink my eyes into an alternate reality, a comforting environment with soft faces and a light so soothing that even the aged and dying feel alive. In this moment's pervasive significance to my survival, I ask questions with the pictures I paint on my face. Raising the muscles above my brows and lips to create the portraits of all the love languages under the sun, I blink again, and I'm gone. The faces fade into granules of sand, a television set bulb burning out into a warm hue of brown blended with white.

CHAPTER ????

Day one stranded is also known as D-Day somewhere else. If we could compile all the stories in the world on this very day, how much sadness would we find? How much happiness is there on a day when a man is stranded, bleeding, and alone on a deserted Pacific island and a band of brothers is slaughtered against the sands of colder shores? Are people writing music on this day? Chewing watermelon-flavoured bubble gum? Selling stocks and trading business? Are people telling jokes and stories in cafés, laughing their hearts through the uneasy notion that there is always terror and torture occurring in this world? Where is the world's population of empathetic deities when these evil days beset themselves upon the earth's crust? The human condition of naivety keeps us all alive until we are forced to feel, and when we feel, we feel hard, we crumble and fall. But until then, we laugh in cafés, chew our bubble gum, and sip our lattes.

Day two stranded finds America on her hands and knees, and day three finds America crawling at the doorsteps of foreign nationals for bids and bailouts. Survival of one is the survival of

213

many, and the surviving sun was my hellfire, the surviving abundance of inaccessible shark-protected food, my slowly developing PTSD. The island provided no shelter or refuge from the intense heat, and my boat, once pearly white in my uncle's dock slip, now dissolved itself into a diving site waiting to be discovered next to my body.

It reminds me that all our bodies are dive sites teeming with stories to be told — stories only the creatures that devour our organs, skin, and fluids will ever hear. The bacterium that consumes our feces has a better working knowledge of who we are than any anthropology expert ever will. We pass our energy, positive and negative, back into a world that is rich with the experience of those sentient beings before us. Our MAOIs, SSRIs, and atypical antipsychotics make our blood run toxic, and we feed this upon our world through our interactions and through our tainted, thinned cells of flesh and fluid, which feed your neighbours' roses as they grow into imperfect specimens with tardive dyskinesia. The divers of the deep and dark, seeking the truth and meaning behind humanity and the faults we never learn from, are the ones we look down on. The decomposers, the street sweepers in postwar Europe — they are the empathetic ones. They are the ones who have seen our decay, the ones who know how we all rot at the end of the day. This is the human existence in its purest form of honest understanding.

CHAPTER ???

I have made a game of setting sticks up at the four corners of the small island I now call home. I run a mile from one corner and half a mile to the other with a stick dragging behind me in the sand, drawing things that from space would dismiss the fears of all humans who struggle to come to terms with the fact that eventually we are all left alone to death. My stick becomes the HB pencil and I become the man under the palm tree, occasionally smiling but more often than not wallowing in the island formerly known as paradise. From another universe, this image is ideal, and perhaps the lucky ones are lost soldiers with no war to fight, left on a deserted island with an unusual amount of fish and fresh water available. At corner three I make large circles in the sand all the way to corner four, and from four half way back to two I draw leaves in the sand, bending as if affected by the intention of the trade winds, bringing life to the view of this image from the stars at night.

When the sky has pitched its dark canopy, I hear bombs dropping and airplanes flying overhead, but it is just the ocean crashing against the sharp yet

215

deceptively fragile reef that provides me with a small sanctuary from danger. My defence lines for my sworn enemy, a species by the name of *Carcharhinus leucas*, a name I don't care to learn more about because I am a stranded soldier terrified of the unknown, terrified in the same way of the nameless faces built into Uncle Sam's campaign. We are all shitting our panties at the cultural variability that we so often reject rather than celebrate. In a world we continue to pretend to conquer, we know all too well through the expression of our fear that we are the true enemies, the intruders, the ones who don't belong. None of us belongs because none of us understand that we have already arrived and that every moment, we are home.

Beyond the preconceived notions and airbrushed postcards, outside of the ocean, tropical deserted islands definitely lack colour. There are only the greens of palm leaves and the varying browns of sand, dirt, and bark that would make a colour-blind man nauseous. There is the blue sky that meets the blue water, stretching out towards a horizon that, in this instance, one would both wish and dread seeing a rescue boat approaching from. Guns will be guns as a displaced American stuck between patriotism and treason will be dead and dead. My drawings have become more extravagant from the sky, and I often imagine John flying into a drop zone a few miles past my island, looking down and seeing my images and wishing he had joined me. I imagine the sounds of war and the taste of blood, occasionally cutting my thumb open on a piece of glass fashioned into a fish hook just to taste the reality of metal in my bloodstream. If this reality is real, I have, for all intents and purposes, officially found my ticket out of the war: I am crazy as fuck.

I make drawings from all four corners because I require some direction in my life, the same reason João Fernandes used the astrolabe even though he realized that the only direction he needed to go was away from what he knew. I draw waves, I draw bombs, I draw SOS signs, and I draw palm trees with our badly drawn island boy hanging from them by a noose. My dreams have become as equally disturbing as my drawings, and I often dream of images that should be impossible to dream of as I have never seen things of such horrendous gore.

I dream of children in furnaces and families stripped and beaten naked to the ground, forced to suck into their mouths the land they had once filled with love and nurture. I dream of blood and constant misery, of limbs sold for experiments and of mustaches that give orders that are met with no resistance. Buildings fall and walls are built that tell stories of oppression and the true potential of human self-destruction. Such insight could not be a reality of my life, though it manifests itself within my dreams night after night, tormenting me and twisting the island into a floating sinkhole stuck between two binding universes.

I wake, fish, eat, and pace around the four corners of my existence with a stick that is slowly shedding its shavings, shrinking from two metres down to one within a month. Frantically pacing about, erasing and re-drawing images of my dreams in my own form of psychotherapy, I attempt to re-process the images I have never physically lived but have seen all the same.

Later into my second month, I make the voyage back out to the boat in hopes of discovering some form of refuge. And I find it.

CHAPTER ????

Rum, whiskey, and vodka — a fully stocked bar that no longer floated but was wrecked like a sunken U-boat stuffed with a belly full of alcoholic beverages to please all sides of the war. I ignored the presence of *Carcharhinus leucas*, stuffing my bags with all the libations I could carry without sinking. The reef was fully submerged as it was full moon with a high tide, making my swim much easier to conquer. I paddled over the shallow insides of the reef, my belly drifting as gracefully as a dolphin on the crest of a wave to safety. Once upon the beach, my feet, unscathed and fully healed from my last attempt to travel inwards to relative safety, I uncorked a bottle of rum and made myself into the artificially happy HB sailor. I sat below the postcard-worthy palm tree gallows, chuckling and grinning to myself at the pessimistic wisdom I had absorbed — only I knew this place was a living hell and not a place of refuge. I would make a killing off of this island once I got home; I knew it and I knew all its deepest, darkest secrets, something that not many people can say about their humble horrible abodes.

First, the rum drained itself like the Oregon winter bleeding into a misty spring, and then the whiskey drifted through my blood like the slow haze of summer grapevine smoke. Fall brought the tongue-tarnishing taste of vodka, and once again I arrived at winter, bones soaked with everything and a general lack of memory for anything that had occurred over the past week. This is the facet of my personal journey that I remember most: the booze. If there had been more of it, I certainly would have required a liver transplant by the end of it all.

I awake with the final drops of vodka vapour expelling themselves from my rubber lungs. I look to the horizon and feel for my HB pencil, gripping the notches I had made down the side of it to count not the days I had been stranded but the number of drawings I had made — an attempt to remember the stages of my own cerebral atrophy and deterioration. I scan my environment and noticed a mark on the horizon, a mark that, at this stage, I welcome with open heart and hands: smoke is billowing roughly one mile out to sea, the distance from one corner of my island to the other.

I fortify myself against all the mistaken thoughts that are attempting to prevent me from entering the water and seeking out this welcomed change. I can feel within my chest the hearts of ancient indigenous tribes who saw João Fernandes stepping onto their soil for the first time; whether he had made it happen or not, the presence of his kind had a profound ability to provide firewater that filled the bellies of curiosity while torturing the spiritual complex of entire generations. I am being invaded and I am holding up a flag that I can't help but paint white. I know that I have to surrender to this smoke monster out at sea along with its black box that will surely allow my country to rescue and then hang me on the doorstep of Marielle's warmongering for all to see.

Properly mentally fortified and without further hesitation, I prepare my life-jacket raft, ignoring the falling tide and using all the remaining muscles I have left clinging to my calcium-deprived bones. I have lost well over fifty pounds and am struggling to breathe at a steady pace. My face is hollow like a felled tree with its insides picked out by termites. My hands constantly tremble with an age that I for some reason felt akin to. My eyes barely stay attached to my slumping facial folds, which remain vulnerable to the sun's streaking images that trace lines of coal fire across my barely living facial expression. My legs are feeble like a man with a day left to live, and my skin has turned hard and leathery despite the hydration provided by the constant humidity of the Pacific. I falter one last time in the thought that society will not consider me beautiful by any means once they find me; I have aged well beyond my years in heart and mind and I fear, for the last remaining seconds of my island life, that I may not make a suitable husband once someday released from prison — if I am lucky enough to serve that as my sentence.

The smoke grows closer and closer and the smell of something produced with manufactured materials makes my genitals spring to life, pressing my buttocks up into the air as my member provides the middle section of my body some extra flotation and distance from the shark-infested waters below. I openly pray that my new PFD will not be the first to be consumed deep inside the open, wet mouth of a shark. Too much tooth is never a good thing.

It is a Curtiss P-40 Warhawk, an American-made, single-person fighter plane with teeth on the front of it that pretend that they are capable of taking down my own foreign enemy, which lay below my seriously hard penis. I once knew these facts of war back when I thought fighter planes and bombers were mere displays of awesomeness rather than killing machines. The defeated aircraft lays on its side, flames emitting from the front section of its Buffalo, New York–made engine. Living in America, it is common practice to see such aircraft fly overhead when travelling south to better surf and often greater military presence; and after all, I had considered war a simple and cool endeavor once.

I swim around the left side of the aircraft, the side stretching itself out to the sea. The smell now shrinks my erection: the burning of American-made human. The wing is slippery, so I grasp onto the protruding metal bolts that act like grips, grips challenging enough for the most experienced of Yosemite rock climbers. Tearing my fingers against the forged steel, I haul my left leg up and over the side of the wing and manage to push my body up into a parallel position with the slanted cockpit. I scramble up and peer through the window, and what I see is a reckoning of my future for years to come.

CHAPTER ??

"John? Holy fuck, Johnny, it's you!" I yell the words as if I am saved. I am not.

"Whoa, man, have I got some stories to tell you, man, fucking crazy. Been surfing waves here like crazy, brah, just like that time we went to Hawai'i, you know, brah? Before I tried on that suit and shit and was that big business man lawyer? Damn, dude, we have some serious stuff to catch up on, fucking, I've been drawing these pictures, man, these images and shit, I think I may become an artist, you know, maybe some Russian satellites caught my pictures, you know? Could sell them and shit. Fuck, so crazy to see you, man! I've had these dreams, man, I swear I saw through your eyes, I saw burnin' bodies and dead people and children in piles of ash, you know? I think I should see someone, is this shit real? I've seen it before, yeah for sure, maybe in a history book or something. That's a wild war, man, can't believe you're here! How are you, man? John? Johnny? Come on, man, stop fuckin' with me. Ricardo, you're such a fucking faggot."

PART IV

CHAPTER ??

You walk through a painted steel doorway, which lends itself to a hardwood decor that describes the type of treatment this facility provides. The brochure doesn't take this lightly, advertising the architecture more than the therapeutic approach used by the staff, a marketing technique that has proven effective time and time again, bringing in more and more candidates; more and more guinea pigs.

A photo of the latest departed rests against a flickering plastic candle, and those throughout the facility wait for their name and photo to be placed on display next. This is not like waiting for your name to show up for the lottery, or like scoring the winning touchdown at the high school football game. It's not the same as having your name called over the intercom by a Spanish maiden at the airport who tells you that you've just been upgraded to executive class because the flight was overbooked. It's more like the sealed, government-issued letter letting your wife and family know that someone high up in some military department is sorry that you were blasted the fuck up in some unimportant mission that served little purpose in ending some unimportant war in an even less important conflict zone. So you wait for your picture to show up at the entrance, endlessly resting in your bed, which folds into a nice little pretzel at the push of a button to aid in your battle of getting out and up to take a shit or a shower.

The nursing staff here don't give a fuck about your deteriorating memory or what it once contained. You could be a world-class citizen or a surfer, a Nazi who escaped the Nuremberg trials or a soldier who fled a war and ended up stranded on some island with a story worthy of the oh-so-desired "#1 *New York Times* Bestseller" copy line on its book cover. They really don't give a shit, it's your memory, not theirs. They don't consider for a second the implications for their own life if they were to let a bit of your memory into their own. Scared of growth and scared of leaving their jobs in these nicely polished rooms. They're even more scared than the next individual who is about to have their face illuminated by that electric candle at the front desk.

A baby breaks the never-ending silence in the residence, a jolt to the stiff air, causing its particles to shift and shape the mood in the room from a dismal weather pattern of grey on grey to a slightly white bloom not dissimilar to the foggy colour of cataracts. Someone's granddaughter's virgin scream initially provides comfort in this room's constant tone of death and dying, yet this screaming quickly turns into annoyance and frustration. Two opposite ends of life collide, and neither of them have the patience for one another. Aren't we all like this, continually shifting between being the child and the almost-departed, frustrated with the crying at one time, dishing it out like a whiny little bitch the next. Memories have an awful way of leaving out the crying child, making us live in a constant nostalgic belief system: yesterday was better, I hope tomorrow offers something similar to anything but now. Unfortunately for those with no memory of yesterday and tomorrow's yesterday, there is only this crying baby.

CHAPTER ???

The air lightens in its hue and gravitational weight, and the white room wakens as I get out of bed with the assistance of some female bedside assistant. I know her only because she knows who she is.

"Morning, Papa." All of the cheer in the world summons me to my feet, and as they press against the cold marble, chiselled from the earth of a foreign land with the hardest of hands, I find myself looking into a face all too forgotten.

"Who are you?" I ask.

"Papa, it's me, Claire. You don't recognize me today, do you..."

She speaks with a melancholic tone that tells me I should know this face, yet my heart won't recognize her because my mind is a tabula rasa, unable to make the connection it requires. I've come to realize in my old age that this is how it all falls together: the heart is only as potent and as accepting as the mind allows it to be. Truly, our emotional attachment to the people, places, and things of this world is dictated by our biological recognition, by the mind's imprint of moments and space in time

229

when something makes us feel to the point where we ingrain that emotional attachment inside our very being. This is a romantic state of being that can only be destroyed by the very organic creation that has allowed humanity to thrive in the face of peril for hundreds of thousands of years: adaptation. Science and psychotropic medications have tried to bring this face back to me, but they have all failed. I think hard with my heart yet continue to prevail as a lost soul before this human.

"I, I'm sorry child, I wish you not to judge me. I'm sorry, I don't— Yes, it would be fair to say that I do not know you, my dear. My name...my name..."

My mind is on fire with the thought that I do not know when the lines on my palms were interrupted by the harsh world they have touched. My scars are permanent tattoos, like maps of a world far removed from anywhere in this universe. My very own existence drives me deeper into the downcast state of being that is so commonly seen on the faces of this world's mentally departed.

"It's okay, Papa. You're *papa* to me, and always will be." This girl smiles at me with a certainty that could break down the walls of Alzheimer's, but no certainty can give consciousness to the heart of a lost mind, and no kindness can ease the suffering of a mind filled with attachments once binding until death and now as inaccessible as the core of the sun. I scratch hard at the inside of my head, like a gardener trying to unearth nutrients from the soil of hell, and stumble away from my bed with a smile that requires more empathy than the world knows to understand.

"Okay, let's get breakfast; I do think I enjoy breakfast." I stand on my feeble legs and hold onto my new favourite memory as she guides me to my place at the breakfast table next to a man on a piano who plays images of stars and galaxies far away. This is a day I'm certain to suffer from once it's forgotten.

"Toast, please, with blueberry jam and orange juice. And the lady, she will have..."

The record skips, but the music continues to play the same distant tune. Outside it is a Celtic morning as the sun shines blood red over the hills of where I am. Has blood been shed, or has war been laid to rest in bed? In my current thoughts I know what we as humans have always fought for.

"I will have the French toast and eggs, please, with coffee!" She speaks in a foreign tongue, and I cannot remember if it is a country I've been to.

"So, how is your year going?" I ask inquisitively.

She laughs with a light disposition about her. "Well, yesterday was quite rainy out so I stayed in, but today is beautiful and I was hoping that you and I could work more on your photo album. Do you remember the one we worked on yesterday?"

I don't.

"Hmm, I'm sorry, are we making something?" I pause and panic. Where am I from? What have I done? And where am I going because of these things?

"Well, let's finish breakfast and then we can work on it, okay? Your doctor says that it's good for you, and me, I want to get to know you better." She speaks honestly and I have to believe her.

Breakfast goes as any breakfast I couldn't remember goes, the sun gradually pulling itself up the sides of the windowpane and spilling its warmth over the fingers of the pianist, who continues to blend his music with my lost memories. The ivory presses down and the piano's hammers trigger thoughts inside me as they pound the strings inside the wood like the fusion of an epiphany and the cascading emotional state of the cosmic traveller I am.

"Blessed we are to have lived." I read aloud the scripture on my tarnished gold bracelet.

"Yes, Mum gave that to you before she passed. You guys, well, you didn't really know each other."

"What kind of a man doesn't know his own wife!" I yell in a fashion that pauses the sixty-frame-per-second life that my eyes can no longer record.

"You, you were a different man than you are today, Papa. I found you after all of these years. It's okay now, you finally have someone beside you."

In her honesty I find a piece of who I am, a man who speaks of storms but never lives through them, a man who leaves his family for blueberry jam and a geriatric home with a nice view. I now judge myself as I would judge a stranger on the train, preconceiving thoughts about who I am and was— and the story isn't hard to read. She had found me in a state, a state of loss I hadn't even known. There truly are angels in this world, I think, placing down my glass and drifting my gaze back over to the pianist.

"Quite a nice tune he is playing. It reminds me of some Hawai'ian melody or something. Do I

know any of the people in this room?" I ask with
sullen eyes and an amber-red complexion, as if I can
repent for my sin of abandoning my family by
beating my lost memory into remembering the
names of a few people in a random room.

"We spoke with all of them yesterday, Papa.
We were all going over our photo albums, looking at
each other's pictures and such. Yours was, well,
yours is a mix of things, and that's, well, that's why
I'm still here, Papa. There are a lot of things I still
don't understand."

Tears aren't as sincere as this girl's tone.

"Well, after my juice and a shake of the dick,
maybe we can begin to discuss this." I find myself
losing grip of my age. Maybe this is the way I used to
talk? Maybe I was the popular jock with the witty
jokes, maybe I was a writer, or a lawyer? I had to be
someone of stature, I was living in a five-star hotel. I
find comfort in this.

"Um, haha, okay…well, let's go do that." She
laughs as if I had just told a nun that I want to have
sex with her thirty-five thousand feet above sea level
so that we can be closer to God, so that he can see
how filthy we as humans actually are and how much
we actually do not give a fuck in the end. These
thoughts affirm me in my identity. Maybe this is who
I am.

CHAPTER ?

"Ayden, good morning, how are we today?"
A man rises above me and claims himself as a
monument in the front yard of my existence.

"Hi," I sheepishly reply.

"Storytelling and scrapbooking begins in an
hour, best brush that fine head of hair, we're all eager
to hear all about your life today!"

I shrink into myself and wonder if he knows
of my incapability to remember whether I served in
the war or I dodged the draft for some distant island.

"I'll do my best."

Young sheep dogs in white scrubs guard the
room, circling all of us geriatrics as though we are
lambs waiting for slaughter. I look to my immediate
left and see a man with a scar carved above his left
eye and a tattoo scribed across his wrinkled skin that
proudly displays the word *moana*. Another man
looks as though he has lived through the hardest of
storms at sea and has come out with only a smile,
knowing that he could have died happily forty-five
years ago. The stories begin to protrude through the
white air and all I have is my eyes, transfixed on the
shimmering silver lining of the windows. Outside an

airplane ascends into thinner air, and I find myself wondering what the destination will look like once that plane lands. Headed far over the western ocean or high over the northerly mountain ranges, who was on it? Who was escaping a reality all too absolute to be a part of? I feel anxiety bind my hands to my knees as they bump up and down like the turbulence of that very airplane. To my surprise, the stories discontinue once they come to my half of the circle. No one asks me to share my story, and I am upset by this, yet relieved at the same time. The group disbands and I find myself at a table with a glass of orange juice and a kiwi and, of course, my muse, this twenty-something year-old girl who for some reason insists I am worth entertaining. I don't deserve this, I believe; from what I know, I don't deserve her presence.

"Say, what are you doing spending your days here with me, anyways? Are you after my cock and money, there, sweet tits? If so, that is a most disgraceful honour, you should know." She doesn't laugh at this, and I'm not sure if I had been expecting laughter or a real answer.

I look down at my photo album and see that there are at least one hundred completed pages. My lips quiver and my hands trace the years, me still subconsciously wishing that I hadn't mentioned my shrivelled-up member to this girl who may end up being my own daughter.

"Jesus, did I do this? Is this my life?" I yell with the amazement of a man who has just seen an alchemist turn metallic birds into gold. There is a photo of a sailboat harboured at a tropical island next to a young man on the cover of a surf magazine; he is surrounded by beautiful women who wear nothing on their skin but their beauty and youth. There is a hazy photo of LA and a man wearing Mexican attire. He is an actor from the 2000s, Claire explains to me. It is all so cryptic — photos from the 1920s, magazine spreads from the 1990s, and finally a photo of myself with the year 2030 stamped beside it, a harsh blow from the dead left hook of Muhammad Ali.

"This, none of this is possible, why are these dates all over the place?" I find myself asking the entire room. The man on the piano stops his rhythmic pounding on the black keys for a brief moment and smiles at me grimly, his lips perched upon a secret that the room is holding from me. Grandsons, fathers, great-grandfathers alike all stare back at me with that same secret upon their smiles from the pages of my photo album. They had all shared their stories — boys, girls, aunts, uncles, grandparents — and like a mental health patient clipping random words of self-affirmation from a magazine, I had made my scrapbook disclose that I have no fucking clue who I am or where my body came from. One hundred pages of blank nothingness disguised with the pathetic photographs of others and their achievements of some form of a life worth remembering. And for the first time I panic — hard. Maybe I have forgotten everything because it isn't worth remembering.

CHAPTER ??

"Did you listen to the others' stories today, Ayden?" The monument now in my mental backyard stands above me like a schoolteacher addressing a young boy about his homework completion and attendance record.

"I was distracted by the airplane in the sky," I say, angered by his accusatory tone while at the same time acknowledging the short length of my attention span. I place my gaze at his feet and follow the trembles of my body as they bounce off the marble floor.

"Do you remember John's story and the importance of finding yourself? You really seemed to find some affirmation about your life in his the other day, Ayden."

I begin to turn red with anger and fear. My fingers trace my cracked lower lip and the pages that potentially resemble this John character.

"John who?" I inquire hastily.

"Look, page sixty-nine, Ayden. Here, this is a photo of John that he has allowed you to have, like all of the other photos the people here at Stino Homes have allowed you to have. This is no blank story, Ayden, this is a collage of life events that were documented outside of your mind. Your internal storage has been wiped like a computer's, but we have slowly been able to re-enact and defragment your life through the evaluation of which neural linkages occur and fire in your brain during the presence of different stimulus or stories, situations, and emotions that others express in your presence. It's called Re-integrated Memory Submersion Therapy, or RMST—a long title for a unique idea that you agreed to partake in when the first signs of what we call Korsakoff's syndrome set in."

"Korsakoff? What is this Russian filth? Some tricky medical bullshit!"

"One of the major symptoms of Korsakoff's is anterograde and retrograde amnesia, Ayden. Your case is special as sometimes your synapses link into abstract patterns and attempt to reconcile a particular history that is logically understandable, but it's not…reality, only an obscure representation of a story that was once lived."

I remain blank inside and out.

"Alcohol," he says.

"What about it? Yes, I could use a stiff drink…you cocksucker…amigo…Johnny what! Yes, a drink, please…make it stiff."

"Alcohol was most likely the etiology. A severe lack of thiamine in your system that could not be corrected by intravenous injections. Your brain has experienced so much cerebral atrophy that your long-term memory is quite literally irreplaceable. But with RMST, we are hoping that, at the very least, your money will be able to buy into research that will provide this young lady some form of closure

238

regarding where she comes from; everyone has the right to know this, wouldn't you agree?" The question is a double-edged sword, this my "synapses" know well enough.

"What is your name? What are you, some sort of witch doctor?"

"I am Dr. Mortenson, Lars Mortenson, and I am a neuro-psychiatrist. And this is Marielle, your mental health nurse, who has been pivotal in exercising your mind, in shaping it and forming it with different stimuli in attempts to re-capture the life events you have experienced. It is a very challenging task, and a lot of money has gone into this research. It's pretty groundbreaking stuff. And because you have little to no ties to your previous life, you are the perfect candidate. We have records that indicate you didn't move much but worked for years outside of the United States before settling down back here. We don't know what you were doing or who it was for, which has been the largest issue of all. But it is evident that someone checked you into this facility and that you came with a large sum of money. We figure that you were most likely working in Japan or Eastern Europe in an underground munitions factory and that you were deployed some forty-odd years ago from your birthplace here in Oregon. We literally have no one who has come forward to help you rebuild your life. Marielle has been the saviour in your story, the messiah who has built up your resurrection. I think somewhere we had determined that religion was important to you…"

"Well, then, who the hell is this twenty-year-old girl?"

"Ayden, it's so lovely to see you lucid today; not every day is like this, you know."

"I asked who she is."

"Claire is your daughter, and like yourself, she knows nothing about your life outside of the fact that your sperm hit her mother's egg — pardon my French, but I think you enjoyed that sort of banter as well. I guess you still do…most days."

Most days? "Will I remember this tomorrow?"

"Most likely not, Ayden. This is distressing, I know, but we hope that by rebuilding your story and repeating it enough times, you will eventually be able to rebuild your memory when the correct types of therapeutic intervention are applied. If we are successful, we may even be given a grant to perform this type of therapy within the public sector.

I bite my tongue but fail to hold back the words. "No one in this world knows my story. I am a forgotten man."

"You have me, Ayden," Claire says, teary eyed. "And I won't forget this."

CHAPTER ?

Where do we decide to go when we live an entire life alone, separated from the human attachment that allows us to prevail beyond our own physical years? I drift in a dream between souls as they pass stories into me and I choose which ones I feel best fit me for the day. Do we really need to experience the world in order to be fulfilled in our lives? Or does watching metallic birds through windows with departed minds help us find peace in the transitory, falsified memories of another? I vicariously live out the rest of my years believing that I have travelled on that airplane, north, south, west and east, past the North Pole and around again. My story is the white air that surrounds me, breathing in the depths of everyone else's lives and breathing them out again day in and day out, each day believing that I have made my living as a lawyer, a writer, a draft dodger, a professional at living. Out that window we all lose some form of what we have done in ourselves, those keys on the piano get old to the hands and ears of the man playing them, but they live on as the sun rises for those of us who fail to reconcile within ourselves that the heart is only as

powerful as the mind allows it to be. I drift like a
vessel and curse like an asshole, no one knows what
the lines on these palms have touched. I may have
been a holy man, I may have been a dead soul.
Whatever story my mind rests upon as my eyes turn
to white will dictate my life's accomplishments, and
for that I find hope in the certainty that I was a man
not worthy of being known, but a man made of
whatever legend my mind rests upon when that
unambiguous wind blows my way.

There are two parts to our subjective realities
of existence:

1) Our thoughts lend to our existence
like the wind guides an ocean swell.
2) Once we lose our conscious thoughts,
we are at the mercy of our hearts, sink
or swim.

CHAPTER ONE

About the Author

Alexander Holt is a Canadian author, psychotherapist, and accomplished musician. He spends the majority of his time searching for remote waves, writing, free surfing and drinking coffee.
Visit him at his permanent address:
www.alexanderholtbooks.com

Works Cited

Heraclitus Greek philosopher (540 BC - 480 BC), Hicks, Robert Drew (Ed.). *Diogenes Laertius: Lives of Eminent Philosophers*. New York: Harvard U., 1925. Print.